THE
BOO

A loving portrait of
an extraordinary man

"*The Boo* represents the best instincts of the boy I once was. It is my tribute . . . to the one man who demonstrated a shining, innate sense of mercy and laughter in the dark land of The Citadel barracks. He was both dutiful and humane, stern and merciful, fierce and infinitely kind. . . . He was the father of the Corps.

"All of us knew he could never quite stop loving us."

Pat Conroy

This book is dedicated with love
To
Elizabeth Courvoisie
Whom the cadets called "Mrs. Boo."

PAT CONROY

THE BOO

TOR

A TOM DOHERTY ASSOCIATES BOOK

THE BOO

Copyright © 1970, 1981 by Donald Patrick Conroy

First printing: November 1981
Second printing: December 1987

A TOR Book

Published by Tom Doherty Associates, Inc.
49 West 24th Street
New York, NY 10010

ISBN: 0-812-58160-1
CAN. ED.: 0-812-58161-X

Printed in the United States of America

0 9 8 7 6 5 4 3 2

Introduction to the
New Edition of *The Boo*

The Boo was the first book I ever tried to write, my maiden voyage on the high seas of English prose, and there is absolutely nothing I can do about it. It is a book without a single strength except for the passionate impulse which led me to write it in the first place. When I open its pages, I can smell the callow idealism and iridescent earnestness of the boy I once was. At times, I open the pages of *The Boo* to reacquaint myself with the kid and see if we could get along today. I think we could, but I'm not sure the boy would be so fond of the man he would become. What an extraordinary arc of difference, fierce as any law of physics, a decade makes. The boy who wrote *The Boo* in 1969 would write *The Lords of Discipline* in 1979. The angle of configuration changed radically and for the time in these ten years. I could not write *The Boo* today no matter how ardently I tried to create the conditions of those sweet incorruptible days when I lived in Beaufort, South Carolina, taught some wonderful kids on Daufuskie Island, was deeply in love with my wife, and thought I would be happy forever. I had not learned how to write then and had not even tried. I had no intimation that my writing and my nature were such inseparable communicants. I only knew that I wrote the language with more facility than other cadets at The Citadel which infused me with no surfeit of confidence over my gift. In the barracks, a proven inability to function in the English language was unassailable proof of virility. Awkwardness with the written word was as natural to Citadel cadets as speed among impalas.

Writing *The Boo* proved one inexorable truth to me: I did not know how to write. That lesson has been of tremendous value, and I've always been grateful that my first book was so modest and naive. It put no pressure on me to match my original effort. It simply told me with its modest voice that I had a long way to go and I would have to work as hard as any writer alive if I was going to say the things I felt in the heart's most private self.

The Boo was the beginning of my education as a writer. I wrote the book in torrid stretches, on weekends and late at night, in white heats of the spirit, in sprints and dashes of a fevered, coltish soul. It never occurred to me that anyone would actually read what I had written, especially with an observant and critical eye. At that time, I had set out to be a poet and I took the proper time laboring over those undistinguished and emotionally torrential poems of my early twenties. It was a happy day for the language when I abandoned the craft of poetry forever. But it would take years to learn that prose required the same intensity and commitment of the spirit. In 1969, prose was something I dashed off quickly; prose, all my prose, was a letter to the world telling what happened to me last summer. *The Boo* was my longest letter to the world; it was also my angriest.

The Boo is *The Lords of Discipline* in embryo. I wrote it because I went back to The Citadel for homecoming five months after my own graduation. I had gone to visit and pay homage to Colonel John Robert Doyle, my faculty advisor and favorite teacher. When I was returning to my car, I spotted Lt. Colonel Thomas Nugent Courvoisie, nicknamed The Boo by the cadets, coming out the back door of his quarters. I had not been close to The Boo at The Citadel, but I had been close enough to know that a sense of both humor and justice was an extraordinarily rare combination to be found in a figure of authority in a military environment. I waved at him and walked over to say hello, walked toward my apprenticeship as a writer, walked toward the history of this book. Unconsciously I saluted him as I made the approach. It is hard to forsake the habits of a cadet in only five months (though my attempts were heroic). We talked with that combination of familiarity and gravity so common among recent graduates and their superiors. Then I asked a question which would change both of our lives. I do not know what my life or The Boo's would be like today if I had failed to ask this question.

"How's life in the commandant's department, Colonel?"

"You didn't hear, bubba," he answered. "They fired me. Canned me. Said I was bad for discipline. They shipped me down to the warehouse. Told me I couldn't talk to any of the cadets. I'm in charge of the cadets' luggage now. I order toilet paper for the whole campus. Supply and Property Officer."

"You . . . bad for discipline?" I asked. To suggest that The Boo was bad for discipline was like proposing that a belief in God was inimical to prayer. The Boo was synonymous with discipline to the cadets of my generation. "Colonel," I went on, "if you ever want to write your story and tell your side, please let me know. I'm living in Beaufort and want to be a writer."

One month later I received a summons from The Boo. I drove up Highway 17 to Charleston and agreed to write the book. We sealed the agreement with a handshake, and that is the only contract we have ever had between us. I did not know how to write a book but I knew how to keep a promise. I wrote the book on bright Saturday mornings in Charleston when I could smell The Boo's cigar in the next room and hear the voice of Mrs. Courvoisie in the kitchen. Six months went by without my producing a single chapter. Then I caught fire and in a single all-night session in The Boo's guest room, I wrote fifty pages. I wrote so quickly, so artlessly; I wrote so slowly, so artlessly. I wrote without guile or craft, but from a simple consuming urgency to tell a story and to right a wrong. I wanted to get The Boo's job back. I wanted The Citadel to understand the egregious nature of its mistake. In researching this book, I learned that if I could tell the whole truth about The Citadel, then I could write an accurate and withering description of the entire human race. The Citadel had its icons and kings, its psalmists and fools. This insight would be of incalculable value when I became a novelist and especially when I began *The Lords of Discipline*. I learned far more about The Citadel while writing *The Boo* than I did during my four years as a cadet.

The Citadel, also known as The Military College of South Carolina, was founded in 1842. The Citadel was very comfortable with the nineteenth century but has had some trouble adjusting to the twentieth. The Citadel sits on the edge of a salt marsh by the Ashley River in the city of Charleston. To the alumni, The Citadel is a religious, not a secular, enterprise and they speak of the school in hushed, ecclesiastical tones that tonsured monks usually reserve for Vatican City. The Citadel inspires more fanatacism per cubic inch than any college I know of, and there are always small-craft warnings around Charleston waters each year during homecoming. The Citadel prides itself on being one of the last protectorates of right-wing conservatism in the country. Its proudest moment occurred when two cadets from the school fired a cannon at the Star of the West, a Union ship trying to relieve the Northern garrison in Fort Sumter. This was the opening shot of the War Between the States and The Citadel's transcendent moment of historical definition. The Citadel was occupied by Union troops after the War and not allowed to reopen until 1977. It is still one of the last places in America where a Brooklyn boy can learn to become a southerner and where a southerner can learn to become a Confederate.

By reading *The Boo* you will become acquainted with the most primitive archeological fragments of a writer's beginnings. But I will say this about *The Boo:* it represents the best instincts of the boy I once was. It was my tribute, my heart-felt valentine to the one man who demonstrated a shining, innate sense of mercy and laughter in the dark land of the barracks. He was both dutiful and humane, stern and merciful, fierce and infinitely kind. The heart of a lion and the spirit of a lamb wrestled for primacy in his high-rulings over our destiny. He was the father of the Corps, the father who replaced the ones all of us had forsaken, and still needed, when we left our homes for college. Like all fathers, he was both prince and tyrant; like all fathers, there were times when he failed and betrayed us. But the mystique of Colonel Courvoisie lingers on indelibly at The Citadel, because all of us knew that he could never quite stop loving us. That love flowed through the campus, an invisible tributary of his advocacy and blind devotion, and there were times when we had to drink from those waters. The Citadel cut the flow when they fired Colonel Courvoisie, when they humiliated him, when they cut down one of their own sons in his prime. When they banished him from life with his cadets it was not merely an administrative decision: it had all the sad elements of the death of unsung kings.

The Boo had risen too high, too fast in the estimation of the Corps. He was more popular than Presidents, generals, members of of the Board of Visitors, and full colonels. He was the prince of our long season, a lowly lieutenant colonel elevated to royalty by the edicts of the Corps' instinct and imagination. He was emblematic of what was best, the very finest, The Citadel could produce. He was fired because of human envy, because his superiors could not bear the devotional esteem in which he was held by his boys. He was fired, and the authorities put out the word among the alumni that The Boo was "bad for discipline." I still hear that dispiriting phrase repeated by alumni I meet in my travels, men who spend their lives memorizing the cold, brittle fiats of the party line. There are some Citadel graduates who would innocently believe anyting The Citadel espouses, who would repeat that the sun was bad for the growth of corn if the Board of Visitors endorsed the sentiment. In the high tribunals of The Citadel, the voice of Galileo recanting can be heard again and again and again. When this book came out, the long war of attrition between myself and The Citadel began. *The Boo* was banned on the Citadel campus for six years even though every penny of the book's profits went to The Citadel. The ban was lifted when they heard I was writing a novel called *The Lords of Discipline*, and it occurred to them that a far harsher book was in the making.

Though The Boo was discredited, he was not forgotten. He kept his mouth shut, did his job at the warehouse, and brought a supererogatory grace to exile. After the book came out, a group of alumni met, started a scholarship committee and raised ten thousand dollars in The Boo's name. The total has risen to over fifty thousand dollars since The Boo's demotion. On what

other college campus in America can they raise
fifty thousand dollars to honor the man who
handles the students' luggage and who supplies
the entire campus with paper clips and toilet
paper? On October 19 of each year, the
regimental band assembles in front of The
Boo's house to play music and deliver him a
birthday cake. Each year, his legend grows,
because The Citadel does not yet understand
the special nature of myth and how it works. In
silence, in duty, in dignity, The Boo has proved
himself their superior. Mess captains require
each freshmen to read this book and acquaint
themselves with the history of Colonel
Courvoisie's tenure as assistant commandant.
By suppressing the history of The Boo, The
Citadel has only served as the reluctant
minister of its survival. The Boo has grown
mystical, supernatural in the minds of the
present generation of cadets. In myth, he is a far
more formidable and capable figure than he
was in reality.

I was going to rewrite this whole book for the
paperback edition. I was going to try to dazzle
you with some fancy hijinks and handstands of
language, use some of the new tricks and
haughty pyrotechnics of the craft I have learned
along the way. But I decided against it. I owe
the boy who wrote this book the kindness of not
condescending to the best he could do at that
time. And it would take too long, and there are
other things I want to write about now. There is
no urgency to this project now; I know how the
story ends. The Boo never got his job back, was
never relieved from his job in the warehouse,

never had a triumphant return into the full embrace of the Corps. He will retire in a year, there will be a parade in his honor for his many years of service to The Citadel, and he will disappear from the campus. But not completely. The writing of this book taught The Boo and me some things about the power of language. Because this book lives, he lives deeply. Because of words, he was not defeated. Because of the innate ability of human beings to be moved by injustice, his fate and reputation are immemorial.

I will leave the book as I wrote it. The changes will be cosmetic or explanatory. I am sorry I was not a better writer when I wrote *The Boo*. But I will tell you this: when I wrote the chapter at the end of the book entitled "Me and The Boo," I heard the resonant, unmistakable sound of my voice as a writer for the first time. I felt the full authority of the writer's scream forming in my chest, felt the birth of the artist in the wild country of the spirit, and knew it was somewhere in me and was deciding it was high time to begin moving out. I have tried to explain why this is not a better book. I hope that in the explanation, you fully understand why I love this book with all my heart.

PAT CONROY

August, 1981

Dedication of the 1964 *Sphinx*
The Yearbook of The Citadel

To select one individual who best represents our theme is the job of the 1964 Sphinx Staff. With great pride and satisfaction we announce our decision to dedicate this 1964 Sphinx to LT. COLONEL THOMAS NUGENT COURVOISIE.

A native of Savannah, Georgia, Thomas Courvoisie entered The Citadel in September, 1934. After three years, he was honorably discharged, returning in 1950 as a veteran student and graduating a member of the Class of 1952.

After his graduation, Lt. Colonel Courvoisie taught at various posts throughout his army career, joining The Citadel faculty as associate Professor of Military Science in 1959. While at The Citadel, he voluntarily accepted duties as the faculty leader in a number of cadet activities. In 1961, he was awarded the Army Commendation Medal for meritorious service.

Appointed to the post of Assistant Commandant of Cadets upon his retirement from active Army service in 1961, Lt. Colonel Courvoisie has the distinction of being a favorite of the Corps while representing the authority which must enforce its discipline. Let the 1964 Sphinx stand as a tribute to one "Citadel Man" whose career serves as a pattern for others to emulate.

Preface to the Original Edition

The Boo gave me only two guidelines when I approached him about this book. "It has to be a fun book, Bubba, and it can't hurt The Citadel in any way." With these two dictums in the back of my mind, I wrote the book, making it as humorous as possible, and making it an honest reflection of the spirit of The Citadel. The book, in essence, is the love affair of Courvoisie for the cadets and his school. The stories within this book were not written maliciously or callously; they were written to show an inside view of the long gray line, an intimate view not often afforded to the general public. The Citadel is quirky, eccentric, and unforgettable. The Boo and I collaborated on this book to celebrate a school we both love—each in our different ways. Proceeds from the book will go to a gift fund honoring Citadel graduates killed in Viet-Nam.

Most of the names in the book have been changed for legal and personal reasons.

Thanks to the following people for their help and encouragement. My wife, Barbara. My daughters, Jessica and Melissa. Elizabeth Courvoisie. John Doyle. Bernie Schein. Tim Belk. Richie Matta. Connie and Larry Rowland. Bill Dufford. Gene Norris. Millen Ellis. Freddie and Lindsay Trask. Bob Marks. Berry Murray. Herbert and Harriet Keyserling. Billy Keyserling. Steve Grubb. John Bowditch. John Warley.

Dr. Henry Rittenberg. Bill Warner. Peggy Runnels. Mr. and Mrs. J. M. Randel. Special thanks to "Tut" and Ellen Harper for their encouragement and love from 1963 to 1967. And to the many cadets who provided these stories.

Scene on the Beach Road

I heard him before I saw him. Call it a Boo-roar. Very loud and powerful. Its effect was immediate. No one moved. Like antelopes frozen on the grassy veldt, paralyzed by the sudden growl of the lioness walking downwind behind the herd; so we stood, too afraid to look around, and very uncertain about the next step we should take. When I finally did summon up the courage to turn toward the direction from whence the shout had come, I caught my first glimpse of The Boo, striding toward some terrified freshman who was trying to keep a forbidden rendezvous with his parents on the beach road. Cigar clenched between his teeth, eyes ablaze with wrath, he was loping in giant steps toward the quivering lad near the road.

The year is 1963 and I speak from memory. My freshman year at The Citadel had begun a week before. Plebe week with all of its irrational terrors had clouded my vision of the world and numbed my concept of self. I was standing in the sand at The Citadel beach house. Only freshmen were allowed this particular day. All about me milled the bleating herd of freshmen who had survived the initial immersion into the system. This day at the beach was our respite. On this day we rested. Even God rested on the seventh day. But my thoughts that day plotted escape: by plane, railroad, passing ship, or oxcart, I was going to get the hell out of the madhouse I had chosen for college. During plebe week I had a senior put a cigarette out on my arm, fainted in exhaustion during a sweat party, and hung suspended from a wall pipe while some daring young sergeant held a sword beneath me. This, I reasoned, was evidence enough that I had made a serious error in my choice of colleges. Unless you have attended a military school and unless you went through the plebe system, you will not fully appreciate my feelings at this time.

Memory differs from experience. Memory softens the features of upperclassmen's faces that once seemed to emanate a sinister and all-corrosive evil. I forget much of the cruelty of that year, but remember most of those deliriously happy moments when the freshmen would gain small and insignificant victories over their tormentors. Memory is a kinder mistress than experience. On this day at the beach, I remember only one face and one sound. I know I complained to a hundred freshmen that day, but I remember none of them. The one indelible image I carry from that day is of a gray-haired, cigar-smoking Lieutenant Colonel in the Army with a voice like a noon whistle. In a single moment of time, he imprinted his face and voice in the minds of every freshman on the beach. This was The Boo.

The Boo. Because of that initial introduction, I did not speak to him for over a year. The power and volume of his voice were unlike anything I had ever heard. I learned that day The Boo was an institution around The Citadel, that he was extremely well-liked by cadets, and that he was their most trusted friend on campus. Good guy or not, his voice could freeze souls traveling to purgatory, and I was not going to cross his path if I could help it.

Six full years have passed since that day. These years have brought remarkable changes in my perspective toward life and people. This book will reflect some of the changes. I have always thought that anyone who writes a book about The Citadel is treading on dangerous ground. She is a world apart. She is so different and so unique in a thousand ways. The Citadel has her quirks and eccentricities like all colleges, but hers seem to be odder than most and much more difficult to justify or explain. And what is humorous at The Citadel is often mere immaturity in civilian institutions. Incidents which find cadets slapping their knees and helplessly convulsed in laughter would not merit a courteous chuckle anywhere else. Even a language barrier separates The Citadel from the outside world. *Knob, plebe*, and *dumbhead* are terms which might be familiar to some civilians, but *shako, press, ERW*, and *pop-off* might as well be written in Sanskrit.* Yet I want to write this book. The story of The Boo is one that should be told. It should be told now before the legend crumbles and disappears from the earth.

The Boo is a special person. This book will prove that. Like the stereotype of the grizzled sergeant whose bark was worse than his proverbial bite, The Boo spent much of his life

---

* A glossary of Citadel terms appears at the back of the book.

barking. He ranted and hollered at a generation of cadets, but could never quite conceal the vast and compassionate human spirit that pulsed beneath the surface. He was not perfect. In the performance of his duties as an Assistant Commandant, he could be a roaring bastard. In his performance of duty, he sometimes seemed too eager to pin the cadet to the wall. He had his warts and flaws. No doubt, some cadets hated his guts and will carry this hatred to their graves. But I do not give a damn about these cadets, just as I don't give a damn about The Boo's flaws. Neither do the cadets he helped, nor the cadets who looked to him as a father-figure away from home. And all cadets looked to him for bright moments in a sometimes gray and meaningless existence.

The Boo played a significant part in my development at The Citadel. He granted favors for which I am still thankful. I think he recognized the renegade spirit which raged within me and realized my frustration in an atmosphere I believed stifled me. In my four years at The Citadel he was the single most important force on campus and exerted a tremendous influence on all the cadets he loved and served. General Mark Clark, President-Emeritus of The Citadel, walked the campus like a retired deity and ignored the general run of cadets. General Hugh P. Harris, his successor, had the warmth of an Amana freezer and never was quite able to achieve the common touch. So it was toward The Boo we turned. All of us. We looked to him for laughter and for compassion. We loved him for what he was and for what he wanted us to be.

This will be a book of praise, casual reminiscing, and moments remembered. I write of a man, his school and the boys around him. Thomas Nugent Courvoisie, Lieutenant Colonel, United States Army, Retired. He served as Assistant Commandant of Cadets at The Citadel from 1961 to 1968. Legends have sprung up about him. I will record both the legend and the fact, or as they say, the man and the myth. The book will be very personal, for I am personally involved. I like the man. But many of the stories happened years ago. Many of the stories that should have been told have been forgotten. Here is a portrait of a man and his school sketched by one who remembers, by one who cannot forget.

The School

The Citadel, to borrow from *Porgy and Bess,* is a sometime thing. Sometimes it seems to be relevant to what is happening in the twentieth century. Other times, it seems like a hopeless anachronism, thrusting its stone hulk into an age that is passing it by. Sometimes the cadet will wonder if he has found a substitute womb —warm, nourishing, and protective—or whether he has simply entered a chaotic world rimmed by four walls that is all rush and disorder. Sometimes The Citadel seems like a world populated by lunatics over which the cadet, as an individual, has no control. Many contradictions hide behind the gates.

One thing is certain: The Citadel is like no other school. It is a proud and dedicated factory of soldiers; a college which stresses patriotism over every other virtue; an eccentric leftover from the Old South when the gentlemen of the manor departed from home to be hardened under military regimen. The Citadel is part of the South and southern tradition. She proclaims with unconcealed pride the role played by her sons in the Civil War. Southern mothers who send their sons to The Citadel believe with absolute conviction that their country offers no finer education. Not only are young men exposed to vigorous academic routine, but they are also required to live by a strict system of absolute regimentation. While other colleges around the nation reverbate from the shock waves of student militancy, The Citadel drifts placidly along, in perfect control of a student body more concerned with the workings of an M-14 rifle than the problems of social consciousness. The Confederate Flag is her indelible symbol. Rockets, jets, and tanks decorate her campus. A war eagle sits atop her main academic building. Her professors dress in the uniform of the South Carolina Militia, a military organization as defunct as Hannibal's Legions. Her president is usually a four star Army General who retired with glorious accolades and a scrapbook of press clippings. The scene is military with all the pomp and circumstance which that term implies. The Citadel cherishes the belief that the more hardship endured by the young men, the higher the quality of the person who graduates from the system. The Citadel devised a formula years ago to improve the quality of men who walked through her gates.

The formula begins with the plebe system. One thing is certain. The plebe system is calculated to be, and generally succeeds in being, a nine month journey through hell. The freshman is beaten, harassed, ridiculed, and humiliated by upperclassmen who concur and believe in the traditions of the school. Under the pressure of this system, the freshman, in theory, becomes hardened to the savage hardships of the world. Life is tough, the system says, and we are going to make life so tough for you this year that when your marriage dissolves, your child dies unexpectedly, or your platoon is decimated in a surprise attack, you can never say The Citadel didn't prepare you for the worst in life. So when the plebe walks into a second battalion on the first day of school, he enters a world so unbalanced and precarious, it takes him the next three years to recover his equilibrium. The freshman is a germ, an amoeba, the lowest form of life. He deserves no consideration for his human qualities, and he gets none. He finds himself called a litany of names and semi-curses: *knob, screw, wad, waste, dumbhead, abortion, nut,* and many others. He is starved at breakfast, tantalized at lunch, and ignored at supper. He does pushups till his arms are heavy as iron; he runs up steps till his thighs grow useless. He has no freedom, no privacy, and no time to study. He cries at night, writes piteous letters to his parents, and bemoans the day he ever wrote to The Citadel. For nine months he marches, braces, and hustles in misery. But at the end of nine months a miracle as strange as birth takes place. The cadet looks in the mirror, and in a moment of supreme madness, decides he loves the place.

To the uniniated, this particular form of behavior borders on the ridiculous or the sublime. It is in this realm and with these cadets that The Boo became a kind of landmark at The Citadel. His was the world of discipline. For it is here that his shadow, looming in the dark corners of the barracks, created a dream kingdom of his own. In his job as an Assistant Commandant of Cadets, he was in charge of meting out punishment for various infractions, both large and small, that the cadets would commit during the year. The job was a combination of many

things. The Boo could be described as part
father, part confessor, part inquisitor, part
detective, part judge, and part son of a bitch. If
you barfed on the president's wife or raped a
Charleston debutante, you would face The Boo
on his territory and under his terms. He
represented law and *The Blue Book*, the cadet's
manual of behavior, the constituted force of
authority, and the power that reigned above the
heads of the cadets. But if he ruled, he ruled
with compassion and humor. He laughed like
hell when he caught some hapless cadet in a
prank, but his gift resided in his ability to make
the cadet laugh with him. Boo was the
representative of justice at The Citadel. The
Boo versus the cadets. These two antagonists
waged furious battles trying to outsmart each
other. Cadets claimed countless victories, but
the number of figures pacing the quadrangle of
Padgett-Thomas Barracks indicated The Boo
was not without his brighter moments. Parry
and thrust, withdraw and retreat, the cadets
never tired of challenging the system. Each side
respected the intelligence and creativity of the
other. Cadets, like prisoners, used every
resource to circumvent rules or to scuff their
shoes on the pages of *The Blue Book.*

This is the stuff of this book: Cadets behind
the stone and steel yearning to breathe free, The
Boo, grand wizard of discipline who held the
great screw in his hand, and the warm, human
relationship that formed between them.

A Matter of Nomenclature

The mother of T. N. Courvoisie, no matter what her thoughts at the moment of his birth, did not name her son Boo. The nickname has made a long journey through several phases, finally arriving intact in its present condition. Some mythical cadet years ago, and forgotten by even The Boo himself, claimed that he skipped campus one night to go to Charleston. On returning, so the legend goes, The Boo spotted him slipping behind the baseball field. Ignoring the order to halt, he claims he was pursued through the marsh and swamp that rim the Ashley River boundary of the Citadel. Looking back at the hapless Army Colonel sloshing through the mud, the cadet later remarked that he looked like a "trapped caribou." Caribou stuck. Tongue laziness and the Anglo-Saxon affinity for shortening words of more than one syllable soon diminished the word to "Bou," and finally to the non sequitur Boo. Since few people residing in the free world today can even pronounce Courvoisie, the name proved beneficial in many respects.

Boo-Language

Boo referred to the cadets as his "Lambs." This shepherd-to-flock analogy pleased the cadets immensely. If you were asking the Colonel for permission to go on a weekend leave, he would usually ask, "What's your problem, Lamb?" and the security of being called that particular animal by The Boo was a feeling hard to describe to outsiders. "Lamb," was not a term of derision. On the contrary, it represented Boo's concern for all cadets and their problems. Whether the cadet in front of him was a fourth class private or the Regimental Commander, he was still a lamb to The Boo and lambs possessed no rank. When one cadet asked The Boo why he referred to cadets as his lambs, The Boo replied, "Because I am the good shepherd."

The word "Lamb" lacks, however, force and emphasis and when Boo wished to be forceful or emphatic, which he did quite frequently, he would use the word "Bum." I only wish that I could attach a tape recorder to this book, one that contained a suitable soundtrack of Boo Roars and Boo Growls and Boo Grunts. When the Colonel said, "Boy, you are a Bum," "Bum" sounded like a peal of thunder bouncing off a distant Alp. It was a loud, slow, rolling sound that crashed from his tongue to your ear like the giant from Grimm's Fairy Tale who bellows "Fe-Fi-Fo-Fum, I smell the blood of an Englishman." Well, the Fum in that line, spoken by huge vocal chords, approaches the range, pitch, volume and intonation of the Boo's rendition of a "Bum."

His voice is important to this story. Its power cannot be underestimated. Bob Marks and I were walking toward Jenkins Hall one morning in our junior year when The Boo let one rip from the steps of Bond Hall. The distance from the two points separating us measured a little over a quarter of a mile. The howl, "Hey you," swept across the parade ground freezing every living creature in its tracks. My roommate instinctively asked, "Is he yelling at us?" On this occasion, the poor lamb who merited Boo's attention was a trifling fifty feet away from the power source. No small voice had he.

A third word to add to your Boo-vocabulary is "Bubba." "Bubba" lacked the warmth and sense of dependency enjoyed by "Lamb," yet it did not have the abrasive quality which surrounded the word "Bum." "Bubba," then, occupied a kind of twilight zone in Boo-language. If Boo used the word "Lamb," chances were benevolence pervaded his mood; if he countered with the word "Bum," the cadet usually could feel the presence of the sword poised over his head; if he merely used "Bubba," a certain equilibrium and feeling of all's-right-with-the-world would descend gently on the cadet. Every young man at The Citadel became a gifted interpreter of Boo-language, a feeler of mood pulses which registered danger or safety in the high-strung world of the Corps of Cadets.

Cadets are people. Behind the gray suits, beneath the Pom-pom and Shako and above the miraculously polished shoes, blood flows through veins and arteries, hearts thump in a regular pattern, stomachs digest food, and kidneys collect waste. Each cadet is unique, a functioning unit of his own, a distinct and separate integer from anyone else. Part of the irony of military schools stems from the fact that everyone in these schools is expected to act precisely the same way, register the same feelings, and respond in the same prescribed manner. The school erects a rigid structure of rules from which there can be no deviation. The path has already been carved through the forest and all the student must do is follow it, glancing neither to the right nor left, and making goddamn sure that he participates in no exploration into the uncharted territory around him.

A flaw exists in this system. If every person is, indeed, different from every other person, then he will respond to rules, regulations, people, situations, orders, commands, and entreaties in a way entirely depending on his own individual experiences. The cadet who is spawned in a family that stresses discipline will probably have less difficulty in adjusting than the one who comes from a broken home, or whose father is an alcoholic, or whose home is shattered by cruel arguments between the parents. Yet no rule encompasses enough flexibility to offer a break to a boy who is the product of one of these homes.

The Boo recognized that not all cadets came from atmospheres which would presage immediate success in the regimented universe of The Citadel. Each day as he sat in his office, chewing great brown cigars and performing the administrative tasks his job demanded, a constant stream of cadets armed with pathetic, soap-opera stories about some real or imagined domestic problem begged and pleaded for favors which only The Boo could (or would) grant. Many of these stories were concocted solely because the cadet wished to leave campus on the weekend. He might want to go home to escape the pressures of the military system, or his girl friend might be coming down I-26 to spend the weekend in Charleston. Whatever the reason, The Boo's office was the only place on campus where immediate gratification of the cadet's wishes could be achieved.

Some of the finest acting in Charleston has not been performed at the Dock Street Theater but in The Boo's office on Friday afternoon. The wringing of hands, the piteous eyes, the voice cracking under pressure, the fevered brow: these were the histrionic weapons of men in gray uniforms confined within the gates of The Citadel, yearning to breathe free. I once heard a cadet tell The Boo that he had impregnated two girls, both of whom were demanding his hand in marriage. Needless to say, he needed an immediate pass to go to his hometown to remedy the seemingly hopeless situation. The Boo, writing at his desk, without looking up, and with magnificent nonchalance, said, "Bubba, you have to do better than that. Why do you really want a pass?"

"Colonel, this girl is coming down. She's beautiful, gorgeous. I've got ten confinements."

He got the weekend leave.

Over the years The Boo became the master of

sifting through the smoke screens and shoveling through the piles of verbal manure the cadets would use as diversionary ploys. If you were going to fool him, your story would have to be airtight. Your acting ability would have to be superb, able to withstand the most withering cross examination, and able to convince the cigar chomping director that there was merit and truth in the gentle lies you were concocting. The more fantastic the story, the more The Boo responded, the more he laughed and needled you. Boys would come to his office and swear their mothers had been raped, their fathers decapitated, their brothers and sisters charred in a fire and never give a clue by their outward demeanor whether their stories were true or merely macabre testings of their imaginations. The cadets were not lying. This is very important. These wild improbable stories were part of a larger structure called "The Game." "The Game" takes place between Colonel Courvoisie and his "Lambs." If the lamb was creative, originated plots and story-lines that involved death, pregnancy, incest, or any other of an infinite number of possible situations, then chances were good that The Boo would grant him a favor. Often he would grant favors for no other reason than the cadet's inventiveness. Mediocrity was the unforgivable sin.

The cadet who approached in the dull prescribed manner of *The Blue Book,* asked for a weekend leave only because he heard that other people were getting them, and waxed sour when cross-examined by The Boo, would usually walk out of The Boo's office prepared to spend another meaningless weekend staring at the bare walls and wooden floors of his barracks room. Unfair? Probably. But The Boo rewarded creativity. In a school where everyone dressed alike, cut their hair alike, walked alike, and supposedly acted alike, it was pleasant to be recompensed for the simple flexing and exercising of the mind.

Background

Why a book about Courvoisie? What is there about the man that elevates him above every other man on The Citadel's campus and makes him remarkable enough to be the subject of a book? What about Mark Clark, the imperious war eagle whose face has graced the front pages of most of the world's newspapers? Or General Harris? Or General Charles Summerall, who was president of The Citadel for the longest tenure? Someone could make a stimulating book by collecting stories and anecdotes about The Citadel's more colorful professors. The great Charles Martin, the hulking scion of the history department with his brilliant parables and classic lectures, his astounding prejudices and his love of rhetoric, could merit a book written by a lover of language and flourish. Stories of John Doyle, "Chinchella" Lucas, Oliver Bowman, and Larry Moreland could form an enjoyable collection for Citadel buffs. The Citadel abounds with figures larger than life who pace within the enclosure of the campus, spewing their ideas in fevered, impassioned lectures, and developing their quirks and eccentricities without fear of reprisal. Memorable figures have always lived within the gates.

So why Courvoisie? It is because Courvoisie embodies so completely the essential ingredients which guided The Citadel in the sixties. It has to do with spirit and attitude. Whenever there was a cadet activity, no matter how dull or torturous, Courvoisie was there watching over his lambs. It was Courvoisie who visited the cadet in the hospital. It was Courvoisie who offered help when the cadet got into trouble. He was stern, yet fair; he was military, yet colorful; he was duty bound, yet human. It was once said of him that if the cadets ever decided to riot, Courvoisie was the only one on campus who could stop them. That was true. Had the full destructive energies of the Corps ever been released in a full-scale riot, Mark Clark would have been trampled. Courvoisie could have met the charge head on, issued a command, and stopped two thousand men in their tracks. If you doubt this hypothesis, then you did not know the psyche of The Citadel in the era of Courvoisie. And it was a strange era indeed. Events on a national scale changed the focus of America forever. It was a turbulent period for America and a turbulent period for The Citadel, who had to adjust to a new and more critical appraisal of the military and military schools. As a microcosm for the greater troubles afflicting America, The Citadel escaped many of the more tumultuous ones. And even though there were changes and upheavals, The Citadel existed as she always has, far removed from the world outside, a place of order in a world of shifts and change. The Boo added security to The Citadel's already imposing walls. Every cadet spoke with him. Every cadet laughed with him. He was a focal point of campus life. Mike Arnone, after receiving his diploma, rushed outside the

Armory, found The Boo, and asked him to sign his diploma. When The Boo signed it, Arnone stepped back, laughed, and said, "Now, I've officially graduated." No story illustrates so well why this book has been written.

Biography

The Boo was born on October 19, 1916, in Savannah, Georgia, the son of Alfred and Anna Nugent Courvoisie. His father ran a filling station and did bookkeeping on the side. The family led a normal, productive existence until Anna Courvoisie died when her son, Nugent, was only eight years old. The Boo and his father moved in with The Boo's mother's people. They remained there until The Boo went off to college.

Two strong influences dominated The Boo's existence during his early years: the military and the Roman Catholic Church. From his earliest memories, the desire to make the military a career was a strong and compelling force in his life. He attended Benedictine Military Academy, a school in Savannah run by monks which prided itself on its discipline and its religious training. When it was time for him to choose a college, The Citadel was a natural extension of his previous education. Only the monks were missing.

He entered The Citadel in the fall of 1934. He did well in the military enviornment. His grades teetered on the B or C level and sometimes dipped below the academic horizon. He was never a candidate for a Rhodes Scholarship, but performed adequately in the classroom until an illness felled him his junior year. He flunked out of The Citadel in June of 1937.

In the summer of 1936, The Boo, following his most quixotic instinct of his life, worked his way to Europe on a freighter. He visited many of the major cities of Europe. In Berlin he witnessed the rumblings and first ominous stirrings of the government which turned into the Third Reich. Hitler and his armies were rising to power, the streets echoed the confidence of the resurgent German nation, and the man whose picture was everywhere would eventually bring Courvoisie back to German soil under far less attractive circumstances.

After leaving The Citadel, Courvoisie joined the Georgia National Guard where he stayed for two years. He was comissioned in the Army Reserve in 1940. At this time the eyes of the world were turned toward Germany whose blitzkriegs were changing old concepts of warfare. The eyes of America turned toward England and suffered vicariously during the Battle of Britain. America suffered vicariously until December 7, 1941, when the Japanese Air Force left half our Pacific Fleet at the bottom of Pearl Harbor.

The Boo's first foreign duty station was Iceland, with the 115th Field Artillery Battalion, a National Guard unit. Life was rather chilly and gray up there, so he kept applying for transfer to units in combat. He was not successful. From there he moved to England in November of 1943. In England he managed to see a pretty Army nurse he had met and liked several years before. Her name was Captain Elizabeth Cosner. They dated as frequently as possible in England. Then she was moved out to the continent. By this time, the

D-Day invasion had put the allies on French soil.

Courvoisie hit France in September of 1944. As it happened the *Stars and Stripes* had received a letter from a 1-A in a 4-F outfit requesting assignment to a combat unit. General Gearhart, of the 29th Division, had written back stating he'd take anyone who wanted to come. Courvoisie wrote *his* letter, and was up with the 29th in combat in less than a week. After three days of combat he was sorry he'd transferred. He and his unit surged through France and into Germany. His division was planning to meet up with Montgomery's forces at the Rhine River. The Germans counter-attacked in a desperate, last-hour attempt to salvage their position. They fought well and hard, twenty miles south of Courvoisie, in what was to become known as the Battle of The Bulge.

In 1945 the war ended. Captain Courvoisie and his pretty nurse, Major Cosner, were married in Liege, Belgium. Major Courvoisie went home at the end of 1945. Captain Courvoisie returned in May of 1946 after having spent forty-five straight months overseas. His daughter Helen awaited his arrival when he landed in the states.

From 1946 to 1950 he was at Fort Sill, the home of the artillery. His son Alfred was born here in 1947. In 1950, he was sent to Georgetown, South Carolina, as an Army instructor for The National Guard. He attended The Citadel with the permission of The Department of the Army. He graduated with the class of 1952.

In 1953-54 he served in Korea. In 1954-56 he was at Fort Benning, Georgia. Then back to Fort

Sill. A year at Leavenworth and finally in 1959 he came to The Citadel as Assistant PMS.

His daughter Helen graduated early from the University of South Carolina, entered the Medical University of Charleston and became Doctor Helen Courvoisie in the spring of 1970.

His son Alfred entered The Citadel in 1965, caught hell for being The Boo's son, received a punishment order from his father, fought a major battle with the quality points, and graduated in August 1969.

Mrs. Courvoisie has been a mother-figure to a generation of cadets. She visits them in the hospital, bakes cookies for them, has them over for coffee, invites them constantly for dinner, and proves the Army adage that the man is only as good as the woman behind him.

Bits and Pieces

The life of every man is a series of moments, passing interludes, and brief fragments which begin with his birth on the hospital table and end with the final benediction of a grim preacher at the open grave. Most events in one's life do not merit retelling; the daily habits of bathing and eating, the morning shave, the reading of the afternoon paper. None of these ennoble or enrich the existence of any man, only make that existence both comfortable and possible. But some moments crystallize behind dark corners, unseen and unforseeable, and spring out like flushed quails when least expected. Some memories linger in a man's mind longer than others, to be savored over, thought about, and remembered as old age approaches. And special people who appear in every life give meaning and variety to existence, by their actions, by the bright effervescence of their smile, or in some cases, by the shadow which darkens and dominates their being. Much of The Boo's time in the Commandant's Department was spent tediously studying demerit lists or checking All-In reports, labor which required time and patience. Yet many events happened which stand out and illuminate the ten years he reigned as Assistant Commandant. Most of the stories he recalls are of the villains and blackguards, the bums and cutthroats who covered the body of the Corps like warts, who mastered the subtle art of *Blue-Book* evasion, and who engaged in dubious battle with the cigar-totin', silver-leafed Colonel who kept them in the strangling confines of his pasture. These are the stories of cadets remembered being cadets and being people.

★

The Boo, as Tac Officer for Band Company, welcomed his boys back from Christmas furlough in January 1965. He bantered with several cadets about their sexual exploits over the holiday. Walking up to Ted Malcolm, the Company Commander, he said, jokingly, but with mock gravity, "Bubba, I heard you got married over the holidays." Marriage was grounds for instant dismissal in *The Blue Book*, even though there have been many husbands and fathers in The Corps over the years.

"Sir," Malcolm answered strangely.

"Did you get married or not?"

"Sir."

It suddenly dawned upon The Boo that he had better shut his mouth as quickly as possible and get the hell away from poor, trembling Malcolm. Malcolm introduced him to Mrs. Malcom and little Kelly at graduation.

★

Cadets sometimes thought The Boo was under the same regimen and bound to the same rules they were. One zealous cadet accosted him at a basketball game and gave him a minor bawling out for attending a Citadel function in civilian clothes, which was a punishable offense for a cadet.

★

This announcement caught Boo's ear as he walked through the mess hall one night: "All friends of Freddie Hack will have a meeting in the telephone booth outside the mess hall at 1900 hours."

★

A. F. Calhoun was a crack rifle shot for The Citadel. During his last year at the college it came out in the Charleston newspaper that he was married. Details about the ceremony were included. He ranted and raved because he had paid a desk clerk at the paper extra money to insure it would not be put in the paper.

★

Suggs Britton, in the school of the big-time operators—a card player who flirted with punishment orders during his entire career, a genuine bum, a cadet who earned a Boo-inspired sobriquet of fourteen carat reprobate—wrote The Boo to tell him about the first job he got upon graduation. He was commandant at a military high school in Florida.

★

During one of the last parades of the year, when the adjutant was reading a list of tactical officers who would not be returning to The Citadel the following year, The Boo walked through second battalion checking for cadets who skipped parade. As he walked up the third division, he heard the adjutant's voice booming through the loudspeakers across the length and breadth of the campus. "Colonel Smith is leaving. Major Samuel is leaving. Captain Adams is leaving," when a loud and vigorous "Bullshit," rang out from a room not thirty feet away from him. Poor Cadet Cludd smiled weakly and accepted the timing of the fates when The Boo peeked in the door and asked gently, "Pardon me, Bubba, but what's your I.D. number?"

★

Young George Durk played the military game well and kept his name free from the debris of excess demerits. He walked no tours and served few confinements, so it was no surprise he died many times when he was driving back to The Citadel wearing civilian clothes and noticed Colonel Courvoisie's green Comet in his rear view mirror. He slumped as low into his seat as humanly possible, peering through the steering wheel, and suffering unspeakable agony as the Comet continued to follow him. The Boo did not see him, but Durk later told him that the moment was the nearest thing to coronary failure he experienced while at The Citadel. Durk became a doctor and practiced in Charleston. The Boo was his patient years later at the Veterans Hospital. In an act of immaculate revenge or pleasant duty, Durk administered three doses of purgative medicine and three enemas to the stricken Colonel. The Boo always thought the smiling doctor was getting him back.

★

Oyster roasts and any other kind of human endeavor which gave pleasure were forbidden to cadets. The Boo broke into a full-fledged roast being conducted professionally by Frank Carter Herst. Herst used garbage can tops to beat them up and was chewing on a succulent oyster when The Boo dropped by to say, "Hello."

★

Romanticism lived in the gilded, nineteenth century heart of Neal Brady, Commander of Company "G." His girl friend, a dripping, drawling, honey-voiced young maiden from Charleston, merited some special celebration or act of adoration when he pinned her at the moss-darkened corner of White Point Gardens. So Brady hid all the freshmen of his company around the garden. As the gallant young Brady pinned his blushing sweetheart, the chorus of silver-throated knobs broke into a chorus of "I Love You Truly." Ah, yes! Old Neal, the last of a dying breed.

★

In 1959 F. P. Canowski's picture graced The Citadel yearbook for the first time. Seven years later it was pictured in the yearbook for the last time. When F. P. finally graduated, an era in Citadel academics, a saga that may well never be repeated and a record that may never be equalled, was over.

★

Life was a serious affair for A. Coplis. The boy smiled infrequently, frowned often, and discarded humor as a relevant part of his life. He walked into Boo's office with his trunk one day. To go along with his dark-cloud view of the world, some cadet who did not take life seriously as hell, crapped in poor Coplis' trunk. Coplis demanded The Boo do something. Boo did. He emptied it.

★

Caldwell Brown was known for his conspicuous and unapologetic consumption. While other cadets suffered in the humidity and heat of summer-school in Charleston, Caldwell walked out to his air-conditioned car and slept in supreme comfort.

★

Though mammas might deny it with vehemence, the cadet away from campus and free from the bondage of The Citadel's iron gates is one part alcoholic and one part animal. Whether a weekend leave or an organized exodus in support of the football team, the gentlemanly qualities of cadet training die a rapid death whenever cadets pass through the portals of The Citadel. In 1961 The Citadel football team won the Southern Conference Championship and received a subsequent invitation to play in the Tangerine Bowl in Orlando, Florida. On the memorable day itself, as the teams lined up for the kickoff, and the cadet cheering section roared encouragement, and the Summerall Guards stood rigidly presenting arms, The Boo saw one of the guardsmen weaving precariously back and forth, back and forth. The debauchery of the night before had proven too much for Cadet Slocum, and even the glint of the sun off his silver bayonet blade and pride inherent in belonging to the Guards could not stem the wave of nausea or impending unconsciousness from crossing over him. Boo inched up behind him and whispered in his sweet, death-like voice, "Mr. Slocum, if you have any hope of living to see tomorrow's sunrise—any hope at all, Mr. Slocum—then you will straighten up and pretend to be a model cadet of the school you represent. And Slocum, I'll be watching you." Almost instantly Slocum became as rigid as a cigar store Indian. The weaving ceased and was quickly replaced by something akin to nervous perspiration. Mr. Slocum is now an Army major with a Silver Star to his credit.

Sam Montgomery, witty but awkward porker from "R" Company, threw his laundry bag off the second division and to the surprise of all observers, went right along with it. Sam was a little shaken, but escaped serious injury.

Mac Coreland used to jump off the second division into the Company pile of laundry bags just for kicks. Mac seemed a little bored with life and this seemed like the most logical way to put spice and variety into an otherwise dull existence.

Tommy Farris came to The Boo's office with tears streaming down his face. He discovered that a good friend of his was stealing from other cadets' rooms. He turned in the boy's name to Colonel Courvoisie, saluted, and walked out of the office, still sobbing.

★

Three senior privates of slovenly vintage took exquisite pride in their wool pants which, according to legend, had been passed down from a sloppy senior to a sloppy junior in an unbroken line for 12 years. These pants covered the limbs of Clammy Sadler, Seymour Farrell, and C. T. Curds, all of whom claimed the pants had never been pressed or cleaned. The legend goes on to claim that somewhere in the nether regions of The Citadel these same pants wander the galleries at night in search of some phantom senior privates who might, with unabashed pride, wear them again.

★

One senior, an acknowledged slob, Zak Sklar, had 95 demerits at Christmas time, which was a hell of a lot of demerits to have, even for an acknowledged slob. The Boo warned him that the gods of discipline would show him the way to the front gates if he passed the yearly quota for demerits. Boo advised Sklar to resign. This would mean Sklar could return to The Citadel the following September. If a cadet is booted for excess demerits, his arse never darkens a sallyport again. Sklar decided to stick it out, became conscious of the shined shoe and the glittering brass, counted demerits like a fat man counts calories, and graduated with his class in June.

★

Joe Sanfort had to walk tours up to Friday of graduation week. The Boo was patrolling outside Padgett-Thomas Barracks when a pretty little girl shyly approached him and asked if she might speak with Joe Sanfort.

"Honey, Cadet Sanfort is walking tours right now."

"I know, Colonel, but we're getting married Saturday and I just wanted to make final arrangements."

"O.K. Honey, I'll get him for you."

★

Raffles flourish in the barracks throughout the year: rifles, liquor, tape recorders, and tickets to rock festivals have been given away as prizes time after time. Raffles make money and most upperclassmen (especially those in Business Administration) know that, psychologically, it is almost impossible for a freshman to refuse to buy anything from an upperclassman. One senior paid for his flight ticket home simply by going to every freshman's room in the battalion and asking for a contribution. A freshman will do almost anything for a friend.

In the history of raffles at The Citadel, and it's a distinguished history, filled with the stories of cadets who made a fortune through the use of their wits, Chuck Haffly rates some type of special mention for creativity and imagination. Every cadet and his mother knows that if you get into your car at The Citadel, drive across the Cooper River Bridge, and head north up Route 17, before you hit the North Carolina line, you will pass the most famous or infamous house of prostitution in this part of the country. The sun does not set on this venerable institution without a stream of soberly dressed businessmen, double-jowled policemen, or lusty-eyed college youths stopping to sample some of the fleshy pleasures offered here. The portly matron who greets you at the door claims that her girls are free from germ or bug, and are inspected weekly by a doctor whose main concern is the prevention of disease and the propagation of cleanliness. At the risk of offending any Citadel mother who reads this book, it is not entirely unheard of for a cadet or a group of cadets to venture northward in search of these forbidden fruits. Cadet Haffly, whose understanding of the cadet psyche must have been considerable, decided to raffle off a night of pleasure to some cadet smiled upon by the spirits. Nor was his a small time venture. Each ticket cost ten dollars, making his raffle the most expensive and ambitious in Citadel history. He found willing contributors to his cause: lonely freshmen who had just received "Dear John" letters from their high school sweethearts, sad-faced physics majors whose thoughts turned from formulas to the sallow complexions of women of the night, and depressed boys who needed some glimmer of excitement to lift them from advanced cases of The Citadel willies. Old Chuck made a fortune. Unfortunately, the winner was a Catholic freshman whose moralistic background and refined sense of guilt took him over the brink and caused him to report the whole affair to the Commandant's Department. Enter The Boo. Old Chuck walked sixty tours.

★

Allen Carlson took no crap from any living man, but dished it out in mountainous heaps to anyone who came under his jurisdiction. Tough and hard-nosed, he worked his way up to become company commander of Foxtrot his senior year. He was hell on knobs. They lined the walls outside his room at night and he would walk before them, a muscled symbol of leadership formed by the rigors of the plebe system. Carlson not only liked to rack knobs, but also had one other idiosyncrasy not usually found in God-fearing, law-abiding college seniors: he enjoyed poaching alligators. On dark, moonless nights in a small motor boat, he would venture out among the marshes, amidst the deafening chorus of insects, and sweep a flashlight across the black waters, until he spotted the two red eyes of a bull 'gator flashing like burning embers in the swamp. A blast of a .410 shotgun and Carlson had spending money to court the bashful maidens of Charleston the following week. The Boo found out about Carlson and the alligators fairly early in Carlson's career, but found nothing in college regulations against it. In fact, everyone knew Carlson poached 'gators.

When Carlson appeared at Boo's office one afternoon, his face an ashen pallor and his hand trembling perceptibly when he saluted, The Boo knew somethng of more than general concern was eating Cadet Carlson.

"Colonel, I need your help bad."

"What's the problem, Bubba?"

"They're gonna get me," Carlson answered, visibly perturbed.

"Settle down, Mr. Carlson, and tell me about it."

Instead of answering, Carlson handed the Boo a letter from the State Wildlife Commission. The letter stated that agents of the commission had caught an alligator poacher in Georgetown, and several stubs in his checkbook had Carlson's name on them. The commission was sending a man to The Citadel to question Carlson about his possible involvement with animal poaching in the state.

"What in the hell am I going to do, Colonel?"

"Pray, Bubba, just pray real hard." As The Boo looked at the letter, he stared at the name of the wildlife commissioner whose name appeared on the masthead of the letter. He took a book from his shelf which listed all the government officials in South Carolina. The commissioner, whose name appeared on the letter had been out of office for two years.

"Anybody hate you, Carlson?" the Colonel asked.

"What do you mean, Sir?"

"Someone has pulled one over on you. You can't tell me the wildlife commission uses stationery two years old to write official letters to crooks like you. I know they have more money than that."

"It's that goddamn knob."

"Pardon me, lamb."

"I know who did it, Colonel. This damn little knob in my company knows some people in the state department. I bet he got that stationery and wrote the letter."

They say that Carlson, an extraordinary racker of freshmen on ordinary occasions, con-

ducted a sweat party of inhuman dimensions
that night for a plebe more creative than most.

★

One of the first bits of propaganda fed to the
cadet, pablum-style, his first year, is the
relationship between the soldier and his rifle.
The soldier treats his rifle as gingerly as a
mother treats her crippled child and shows it
the same respect a parish priest gives a visiting
bishop. In The Citadel's entire history, only one
cadet, B. M. Schein, has ever walked into the
Commandant's Office and said, "I will not be
turning in my rifle. I can't find it." Poor B. M.
had lost the weapon, simple as that. He could
not find the damn thing and he had searched the
entire campus. Since the loss of an M1 and
matricide are roughly comparable at The
Citadel, B. M. looked at Citadel walls for six
long months and his feet burned second battalion for 120 tours.

★

Larry Orb was a cadet of questionable
character. A cadet accused Orb of an honor
violation. He was tried and found innocent
because of some technicality involved in the
case. Orb beat up the cadet who made the ac-
cusation the day after the trial and then
received 10 months restriction and 120 tours.

★

The Boo calls Carl Mazzarelli the nearest
thing to a full-fledged gangster The Citadel ever
welcomed to her gates. He once went to the
company bulletin board, saw his name men-

tioned prominently on the demerit list, flew into an uncontrollable rage, ripped the whole bulletin board off the wall and hurled it to the quadrangle twenty feet below him. On another occasion, The Boo saw a figure dart from a line of cars, after taps, near third battalion. Boo did not give chase. One lesson he learned early was that old hearts do not function as well as young hearts during foot races. He merely went down the line of cars until he came to one whose engine was warm. He took the number off the car's sticker, checked the records in his office, and made an extremely cordial phone call to Cadet Mazzarelli the next day.

★

A gargantuan jock who stood like an anvil at left tackle during the football season went up to the head of a department and practically begged to take seven subjects his senior year. The department head persisted in knowing exactly why he had to take seven subjects. The jock, A. W. Reynolds, answered, "Because I'm married, Sir." The teacher turned him in and Reynolds was expelled.

★

Once upon a time there was a basketball player who rose to the rank of Captain in the Corps of Cadets, a rare blend of athlete and soldier like Conroy. He also performed brilliantly in the classroom. Many people turned to him whenever any discussion of model cadet arose and pointed out that he excelled in every phase of cadet activity. The night before graduation, this admirable, triple-threat cadet partook of the bottle and the vine a little too vigorously. On the way to receive his diploma, he vomited into a little bush beside Bond Hall. He was carried unceremoniously back to barracks. He received his diploma later. This vomiting trooper is now an emiment professor in the Business Department of The Citadel.

★

The name "Stindle" means very little unless you come from Union, South Carolina, or thereabouts. Then you'd know the Stindles had money flowing from the glove compartment of their blue Cadillac which sat in front of a house built for the landed gentry. Them Stindles owned Union. Landon Stindle came to The Citadel and became an outstanding cadet. In the early sixties, he was regimental commander. He went with a beautiful girl for four years and planned to marry her when he completed his three-year stint in the Marine Corps. He left his girl friend under the benevolent care of his best friend, Jim Rheinhart. Jim took excellent care of Stindle's girl. He married her.

★

One night while making his appointed rounds of the barracks, The Boo had paused in a freshman room to give them merits for outstanding room during study period. While he was there, a knock sounded on the wall in the next room, the universal signal for young knobs to go scurrying to the service of indolent seniors. Boo left the room and cracked the door of the next room and said meekly, "Yes, Sir."

Tod Dood sat comfortably with his back to

the door, his feet propped on his desk, looking over some papers he had written.

"Bring the cream in, Dumbhead, the coffee's ready," Dood said without looking up.

"Thank you, Bubba. That's all I need."

Dood buried his head in his hands and still without looking up or turning around, pleaded, "Colonel, you can do anything you want to me, but please don't tell anyone how you caught me."

★

Daryl Butker, in a futile attempt to popularize the troubador's art on The Citadel campus, would waltz into Colonel Courvoisie's living room, strap on his guitar and sing his ERW's, his explanation required written, to the Colonel.

★

Another music lover, Caleb Winston, went AWOL his freshman year and took nothing with him but his two guitars. He left toothbrush, underwear, and picture of his girl at The Citadel, but his two damn guitars went over the wall with him.

★

During June Week of his freshman year, Denny Copester was creeping back on campus at two in the morning when a campus night watchman ordered him to halt. Since the general run of watchmen at The Citadel are selected at random from the dregs of mankind, Copester decided to make a run for it. The guard who took his job rather seriously, fired a warning shot over Denny's head. Denny prudently fell to the earth. The Boo gave him a punishment order of 3 months restriction and 60 tours and fined him 53 cents for the round of ammunition the guard wasted firing the gun.

★

Boo often checked the zoo area, otherwise known as "A" Company where the towering jocks grazed in relative tranquility. One night in early spring he saw a room with the lights out, opened the door, flipped the lights on, saw two figures in bed, turned the lights off, and closed the door. As he was taking the two cadets' names off the door, he could not shake the persistent feeling that something was just not right. He opened the door again, cut on the lights once more, walked over to the beds, and threw back the covers. Dummies, complete with wigs, occupied the beds. Cadets Whitner and Reyt, imbibing freely at the Ark, a neighborhood bar, returned to The Citadel late that night to discover 120 tours awaited them to walk in their leisure time.

★

A senior mess-carver learned that a freshman at his table was allergic to tomato juice. He made the freshman drink nine glasses that same morning. The freshman required emergency treatment at the hospital. The Boo and the Commandant's Department recommended the senior be shipped, but he was given 2 months restriction and 40 tours instead. This was one of the cruelest violations of the Fourth Class System The Boo heard about during his reign as Assistant Commandant.

★

Boo's association with the band and its members would constitute a book in itself. But one of his habits which eventually became tradition was his solemn march behind the line of bagpipers dressed for parade. On this march, he lifted the skirts of the pipers to make sure they were wearing drawers. J. W. Howt used to exchange wisecracks with The Boo every Friday when the ritual resumed.

"Do you like what you see back there, Colonel?"

"Howt, everything I see back here looks better than your face."

Each Friday, The Boo and Cadet Howt fired verbal fusillades at each other. What The Boo didn't see was his photograph pasted onto Howt's drums, and as the parade began, and the cutting session ended, Howt marched onto the field beating the hell out of his major antagonist.

★

Alvin Reet and W. J. Milder, two of the first cadets who made the discovery that The Boo could be a leaping son of a bitch on occasion, burned a cross on his front lawn.

★

Bill Winters lingered too long in the barracks after graduation, possibly reflecting on his long and distinguished career as a senior private and bum in residence, when The Boo, tired of waiting, locked the gate and gave Bill the distinction of being the only cadet ever locked in the barracks on the last day of school.

★

Before a West Point football game, the Colonel got a phone call from a man named Goldman who said he used to be a private in "G" Company and needed tickets for the ballgame. When The Boo couldn't place him at first, Goldman said, "Hell, Colonel, you remember me. I was the only Jew in your company."

"Sure, Bubba."

He got the tickets.

★

R. V. Gordon studied like hell and had the grades to prove it. He ranked one in the political science department and fully expected to represent The Citadel at a political science convention at Annapolis. He came to talk to The Boo one afternoon, very frustrated and bitter, and told him his department had chosen to send a man with rank, instead of a senior private. Something like the image of The Citadel was involved.

★

Mickey Rollins and Ed Zurowski rated the titles of first class bums, but both of them were pretty good students. Both of them liked to have a good time and play the *la dolce vita* bit. They were playing leap frog one day on the beach, when Mickey leaped too far and landed on his head. The broken neck sustained in the fall nearly killed him. It was damn close for a while, but he made it.

★

Theoretically, Carey Tuttle would graduate in January if the gods continued smiling warm smiles upon him. Some god quit smiling and The Boo caught him selling hot popcorn on a chilly night in early January. The month restriction would prevent him from graduating, so he begged The Boo to give him some chance of escape. The Boo slapped him with a fine of $50.00 that would sweeten The Citadel's treasury. He paid off forty-two dollars. Hereby, let it be known that Carey Tuttle still owes eight dollars.

★

Jimmy Spur's father was a classmate of The Boo's at The Citadel. Jimmy stayed in trouble with the law during his entire career at The Citadel. He and The Boo had several disagreements and The Boo nailed him with a punishment order. Later, some merchants downtown complained that Jimmy owed them a lot of money. Boo co-signed a note of a few hundred dollars so he could pay his bills.

★

One thing which irritated upperclassmen of the 1960's was the sight of perspiration stains ringing the armpits of obese freshmen awaiting inspection at noon formation. Whether this was because of television's influence with its ubiquitous commercials extolling the virtues of desert-dry underarms or simply some hang-up which became generalized throughout the Corps, no one really knew. The mother of David Wellman stormed into The Boo's office one day. She was a large and effusive woman with her exaggerated features heavily made up. She begged and exhorted The Boo to keep the hungry pack of upperclassmen from devouring her fat, sweating little boy, David. She had sent him deodorants, both stick and spray, special odor-killing soaps, powders, and even deodorant pads. Nothing worked. Big, ugly perspiration stains still plagued him at noon formation. She wept copiously and as she told the tragic story of her son, she did not notice The Boo on the edge of hysteria, trying to keep from laughing as he watched the purple rivers of mascara drip down her face with every tear.

★

When Larry Wolf walked up the flight of stairs in Jenkins Hall and walked into Courvoisie's office, it was easy to tell that something was eating the kid.

"Colonel, I have something to tell you."

"What is it, 'Wolf'?"

"Colonel, I just have to get married. I have to. I love her and she loves me and we just have to get married."

"That's fine, 'Wolf'. But The Citadel's no place to be married. Your wife can't be with you. There's no sense of companionship. You'd miss the hell out of her during the week, break barracks every time you got the chance, and get yourself into a lot of trouble."

"I know, Colonel, but we're in love and there's nothing else we can do."

"O. K. Good luck, Bubba, whatever you do."

Several weeks later Larry returned to his office with tears in his eyes and said, "Colonel, something terrible has happened. I have to go home right now. I can't wait for the weekend."

"O. K., Bubba, you have twenty-four hours."

The Boo later learned that Larry's girl had married another guy from their home town.

★

Pete Reston and Jerry Bester engaged in a kind of psychological warfare against each other their entire senior year. Jerry, being a cadet major, held a distinct advantage on the disciplinary battlefield. Pete, fighting with limited resources, helped stimulate Jerry's intellectual life by ordering over sixty magazines and signing Jerry's name to the purchase order.

★

In February 1966 Colonel Bosch, the Comptroller, called Colonel Courvoisie and asked him to hunt a cadet for him. Bosch went on to say that $47.50 worth of senior business books were charged to a freshman's I.D. card. The freshman had left The Citadel in November. When they punched a few holes in the proper places and ran a card through the computer, Bosch and his assistants discovered that all seniors in the business department had bought books except three. "Is there anything you can do to help us, Colonel?"

"Yes, Sir, I believe so."

Boo went to second battalion and asked Allan Wudie, Band Company Honor Representative, to walk around campus with him on some business which might involve the honor court. Wudie complied. Boo had three names on a sheet of paper.

The first name belonged to a cadet who lived on the top gallery of second battalion. Cadet North, a second lieutenant in the corps, popped to attention when Colonel Courvoisie and Wudie walked into his room.

"At ease, Bubba. Could I see the books you're using in your major field this semester?"

"Yes, Sir. Here they are, Sir. Why are you looking, Sir?"

"Just checking, Bubba."

Six brand new business books lined the top shelf of his bookcase. Cadet Wudie carefully wrote the name of each book on a piece of paper. Before they left the room, Cadet North asked again, "Have I done anything wrong, Colonel?"

"I don't know, Bubba. I was just told to check some books. Good Morning."

The next cadet was asleep on his bed in fourth battalion when The Boo walked into the room. His two roommates who were studying leaped from their seats, but Harold Criddle, oblivious to the presence of danger lurking in his room, slept on in undisturbed slumber, until The Boo let out a roar for Harold to hit the floor. Blanching and stuttering in surprise, Criddle stood in his underwear at rigid attention.

"Where are your senior business books, Bum?"

"Well, Ah, Colonel, Sir. Well, I haven't picked them up this semester yet. You know, I just wanted to save a little money. Thought I'd use my friends' books just to get by."

"Bubba, do you realize this college requires you to have textbooks so you can extract every morsel of knowledge from your courses to help you in your future life?" "Yes, Sir."

"You pick your books up tomorrow and bring me the receipt for their purchase."

"Yes, Sir."

Wudie and The Boo then climbed the "O"

Company stairwell and found the room of Preston Grant empty of occupants. The Boo yelled down to the O.G. on duty, "Find me Cadet Grant and get him to this room immediately." So the frantic O.G. placed calls all over the campus, sent his orderlies on scouting missions, searched Bond Hall, the library, the pool room, and finally found him watching T.V. in the Senior Lounge.

"The Boo wants you in your room right away," an orderly said.

"What in the hell did I do this time?" Preston intoned, as he broke out of Mark Clark Hall in a sprint and did not slow down until he stood before The Boo breathless and still wondering what crime he had committed.

"Mr. Grant, show me your senior business books you bought this semester, immediately."

"Colonel, I just haven't picked them up yet. You know with graduation and all how important it is to save money and stuff. I've got one book, but it belongs to a friend of mine. We've got a test in that course tomorrow."

"Bubba, you prove to me in my office that you bought every God-blessed book your department requires, understand?"

"Yes, Sir."

As The Boo and Cadet Wudie walked out of fourth battalion, they were met by Cadet North in the sallyport. He once again asked the Colonel a question.

"Could you please tell me why you were checking those books, Sir?"

"Because I was told to check them, Bubba."

"Should I call my father, Colonel?"

"Do you think you ought to call your father,

Bubba?"

"Yes, Sir. I know why you're checking the books."

The cadet was a senior planning to get married in June and making the Air Force a career. Friends of his told The Boo the boy was so intense about saving money that on the long drive to his home in Virginia on Christmas furlough, North drank only a glass of water while the other cadets in his car loaded up on hamburgers and milk-shakes. His Air Force career was sold for $47.50; he left The Citadel the next day.

★

The appearance of the Clarey twins made them easy to underestimate. Both were squat and dumpy, red-headed and funny as hell. They worked as a team in anything they did on campus, and even though one was basically an extrovert and the other more reflective and an introvert, when they got together they clicked like blinking lights together. You could shut one of them up and the other one automatically started chattering like a sarcastic rodent. They stood beside each other in the same squad, lived in the same room, and ate together on the same mess. Everyone gave the Clarey twins a wide berth, and few people wanted to incur the wrath of either one since that entailed warfare with the other, too. They wisecracked and clowned their way through four years of The Citadel, but they saved their most memorable performance for graduation day.

Graduation is one of those serio-happy days when the Generals dress more ostenatiously than usual, when the Professors look more forbidding and learned than usual, and when the cadets fidget more often than usual. Boring speech would follow boring speech as some unknown orator would deliver the graduation address saturated with phrases about youth being the key to tomorrow's world and other such profundities. After the speeches, Colonel Hoy would begin calling the names of the graduates. They would walk across the stage, individually, shake hands with General Clark with one hand, and receive their diplomas with the other. Graduation was nice. General Clark liked it. The Board of Visitors liked it. Moms and Dads like it. And the Cadets hated it, for without a doubt it ranked as the most boring event of the year. Thus it was in 1964 the Clarey twins pulled the graduation classic.

When Colonel Hoy called the name of the first twin, instead of walking directly to General Clark to receive his diploma, he headed for the line of visiting dignitaries, generals, and members of the Board of Visitors who sat in a solemn semi-circle around the stage. He shook hands with the first startled general, then proceeded to shake hands and exchange pleasantries with every one on the stage. He did this so quickly that it took several moments for the whole act to catch on. When it finally did, the Corps went wild. General Clark, looking like he just learned the Allies had surrendered to Germany, stood dumbfounded with Clarey number one's diploma hanging loosely from his hand; then Clarey number two started down the line, repeating the virtuouso performance of Clarey number one, as the Corps whooped and shouted their approval. The first Clarey grabbed his diploma from Clark and pumped his hand furiously up and down. Meanwhile, his brother was breezing through the hand-shaking exercise. As both of them left the stage, they raised their diplomas above their head and shook them like war tomahawks at the wildly applauding audience. No graduation is remembered so well.

★

The Regimental Executive Officer of an intentionally forgotten year came up to The Boo after military science class and asked The Boo for an "A."

"Why do you need it, Bubba? To graduate?"

"No, Sir, I want to make gold stars."

"Hey, Bubba."

"Yes, Sir."

"Drop living dead."

★

Many future pilots seem eager and gung-ho, but few wanted to fly as badly as Bill Talbert. He was doing extremely well during his eye examination at Charleston Air Force Base, until the doctor made the fairly relevant discovery that Bill was wearing contact lenses.

★

When Rick Lovefellow took off his shoes and socks and danced like a sugar plum fairy through field and grass reciting Keats and Coleridge to a group of cadets, no one seemed to think it strange or extraordinary because it was Rick Lovefellow doing it and everyone knew Rick Lovefellow was crazy as hell anyway. Boo shouted at crazy old Rick Lovefellow for four years and old Rick just grinned that huge grin which spread all over his face and then seemed to ripple through any crowd he might have assembled around him. Boo once caught him wearing a pair of shoes that looked like they might have been taken from a dead soldier's feet after the battle of Tippecanoe. Terrible shoes with big gaping holes exposing toes and metatarsals to the world. Of course, Rick had put several Johnson's bandaids over the holes and painted them black, but still the finished product did not deserve to grace Rick's feet at a Saturday morning inspection when all the earth expected cadets to shine like grounded stars. The Boo found him that day and roared at Rick with his turbo-jet voice and crucified him without using nails, and humiliated him in front of an entire battalion, and Rick just grinned.

On another occasion Rick slouched his way across the parade ground during summer school, wearing bleached, torn blue jeans which Rick thought gave him a sexy, symbol-of-the-sixties look. Boo's dress edict of the summer declared that no cadet would wear blue jeans on campus. Boo's voice boomed across the parade ground and halted Mr. Lovefellow dead on the spot. "Mr. Lovefellow, don't you realize you are wearing blue jeans on campus?"

"So I am, Colonel. So I am."

"What are we going to do about it, Bubba?"

"Let's let it go by this time and play the game some other day, Colonel."

"Give me your pants, Lovefellow. A cadet cannot be seen walking around campus wearing blue jeans."

Rick, a little more serious now, said,

"Colonel, Sir, pardon me, but it would be a hell of a lot better than a cadet walking around in his underwear."

"Shed 'em, Bubba."

So several cadets saw Rick Lovefellow racing for first battalion, his bare legs exposed to the harsh Charleston sun and his buttocks covered by a pair of new fruit of the looms, but they just nodded and noted that Rick Lovefellow was still crazy as hell and didn't think too much more about it.

★

At the graduation review of 1968, The Boo was shaking hands with the band seniors as he was accustomed to do. Something caught his eye about thirty yards down the line of seniors. Something odd. He walked down the line and found a grinning Rick Lovefellow sporting a huge gold medallion about the size of a volley ball suspended from his neck by a gaudy red ribbon a foot wide. Boo slowly untied the medallion and whispered soft thunder into Lovefellow's ear, saying, "You Bum, if you want to sit in your room until 0900 hours Saturday morning, you just look like you're going to pull one more stunt like this."

The Boo turned away from Rick and spotted Colonel and Mrs. Lovefellow standing about twenty feet behind their son. The Boo walked up to Mrs. Lovefellow and growled, "Does this belong to your son, Madame?" She swore she didn't know the lad.

★

Basil Rathbone, English actor who won his major fame by playing Sherlock Holmes in the movies, came to The Citadel to deliver Shakespearean readings as a tribute to the 400th anniversary of the Bard. The salute guns awakened him at three in the morning and he thought it strange, the customs and traditions adhered to by these military colleges. Basil was not the only person awakened. A senior private in first battalion woke up and looked out in time to see cadets going in the vents on the north side of the second battalion. The next day he told The Boo what he had seen. Colonel Courvoisie went down to second battalion and checked the vents which led under the barracks. On one vent he found a false, wooden bar, painted to match the other bars, which was removable. The Boo entered the vent, saw some footprints and followed them to a band company room. He took the room number, then left the barracks. He called the cadets who occupied the room later that day.

"Bums, I found some footprints leading to your room from an outside vent. Now, unless you come up with some other names, you are going to get 3/60 for firing the salute guns at three in the morning." 3/60 was 3 months restriction and 60 tours.

"But, Colonel, we didn't do it."

"I know, Bubba, but you know who did."

Several hours later, the two cadets who had interrupted Basil's sleep, Neck Selzner and Frank Rabon, turned themselves in and asked for mercy.

★

While checking summer school barracks, Boo walked into an empty room and found two three-foot alligators with their mouths taped shut, wandering around the floor. With a roar that awoke newborn infants in Roper Hospital, The Boo stood from the top gallery and said, "Get these damn alligators out of here before I throw them off the top division."

The message carried all the way to Chris Carraway who was attending class at the time, but who hurried to the barracks to retrieve his 'gators before they became airborne.

★

Wayne Wolski, a Cadet who never graduated from The Citadel, called Colonel Courvoisie one Wednesday night after he left school and said, "Colonel, I want you to be godfather for my child. I don't want anyone else, understand me?"

"O. K. Bubba, don't get riled, nothing's wrong with your kid, even if his father is a Bum."

The Story of Mr. Bison

In 1963 Eddie Teague recruited a boy from Mobile, Alabama, who had the potential to become an outstanding interior lineman for The Citadel's football team. Because of a nineteen inch neck which seemed to blend imperceptibly into his massive shoulders, he was dubbed "Mr. Bison" by other members of the squad. Some of them had met this neck head-on in a fierce scramble on the practice field. Mr. Bison handled himself well. In the violent world of football, where success was measured by the number of bodies strewn in your path, the boy from Mobile with the stove pipe neck would easily match the best of them. The Corps became accustomed to cheering the quick, sharp tackles made by the Bison in his relentless pursuit of enemy ball carriers. He lettered in his sophomore year. Things looked good and Mr. Bison wrote his mother that he had picked a fine school.

Things had not always been good. His childhood had been a hard one. His father's connection with the Mafia caused a great deal of dissension between his parents. He spent his early years watching a procession of surly hoods parade through his house. They seemed oblivious to the arguments that inevitably puncutated their visits. The arguments eventually caused a rift which led to separation and divorce. Mr. Bison's father, freed from family ties, became a drifter and faded out of his son's life forever. The mother assumed responsibility for raising the family. The hard times came. Poverty entered Mr. Bison's life. He watched his mother come home from work, fix dinner and fall into bed exhausted. This was a daily ritual. Yet no matter how hard she worked or how exhausted she became, there still was not enough food, nor clothes, nor anything. Some of the kids at school made fun of Mr. Bison's clothes, but not for long. His quick temper would flash and the growing bison would silence his antagonist or get the hell beat out of him trying. He started hanging around the tough kids at school. They were kids like him who didn't have enough money. They came from the poor section of town and their bond was the hard affection of alienated children painfully aware of their poverty.

In Junior High School, Mr. Bison discovered football. On the field he learned that some of the hate inside him could be released by driving his shoulder into the gut of an opponent or by racing downfield and splitting a defensive half-back in two with a well-executed body block. And people praised you for it. Teachers didn't yell at you and the principal didn't suspend you. Everyone cheered. The harder you hit someone or the more savagely you tackled someone, the louder the applause became. In a world of contradictions, Mr. Bison found the niche that would carry him from high school in Mobile, Alabama to the more spacious arena of Johnson Hagood Stadium in Charleston, South Carolina.

In the spring of 1964 the O. G. in Number

Four Barracks was roused by a cadet who saw something suspicious occurring in the parking lot adjacent to the tennis courts. They alerted the Officer in Charge and the group went out into the dark to investigate. They caught two cadets with a long hose and an empty gas can. The gas can was empty, but the intent of siphoning gas was obvious. They were both charged with honor violations and summoned to appear before the Honor Court. One of the boys was familiar to the O.C. The thick neck and strong body had impressed him the previous football season. He had watched this man tackle a Furman halfback on The Citadel fifteen yard line so hard that the ball was jarred loose and recovered by a Citadel player. He had seen him before, but it was the first time he had spoken to Mr. Bison.

Colonel Courvoisie had spoken often to Mr. Bison. Passing him on campus, The Boo would ask him about the football team or about his grades. Boo had similar conversations with hundreds of cadets each day. Whether giving you demerits for unshined shoes or standing by Bond Hall waiting for cadets late to class, he always talked to the boys who passed him. He forgot most of these conversations as soon as he had them. It was the cadets who remembered them. Mr. Bison remembered them.

The trial proved to be one of the most controversial in the history of the Honor Court. Could an honor violation be committed by intent alone? Should planning to steal be punished as severely as the act of stealing itself? All of these questions were debated by cadets all over the campus. Even the members of the honor court could feel the pressure mounting as all eyes turned toward the third floor of Mark Clark Hall for the trial which would stand as a test case, a kind of reference point from which later honor courts would embark. Joseph Dickson, a member of the court, later said to his brother that he had never been so torn by a decision as the one rendered that night. The court unanimously decided that Mr. Bison and his companion were guilty of an honor violation. There was no recommendation for leniency. According to the rules, Mr. Bison had to leave The Citadel campus forever in less than twenty four hours.

Colonel Courvoisie's most detested job was supervision of those cadets found guilty of honor violations. It was his appointed task to make sure the cadet left as quickly and quietly as possible. He had heard of the court's decision before Mr. Bison came to see him the next morning. Mr. Bison was shaken and even though he tried to be stoical, Colonel Courvoisie could see the anxiety etched across the boy's face. The nineteen inch neck seemed little protection against the uncertainty of the future.

Colonel Courvoisie spoke first. "There's not much I can say, Bubba."

"I know, Colonel, there's not much I can say, either," he answered.

"You know General Clark will write a letter to get you in another school, don't you?"

"Yes, Sir. That's nice of him."

"Don't worry, Mr. Bison. Things look bad now, but you'll come out O.K."

The Boo had listened to other cadets talk about Mr. Bison's background, the economic deprivation of the early years in Mobile, Alabama, and the derelict father who left home. He had heard about the life the boy led before football had lifted him into The Citadel. He knew some of the circumstances. He understood.

"Mr. Bison, can I help you—lend you some money?" the Colonel asked gently.

"Colonel, I sure could use thirty dollars."

The Boo wrote a check and gave it to him. Mr. Bison extended his hand. They shook hands.

"Good-bye, Colonel, and thanks."

"Good-bye, Mr. Bison. Good luck to you."

When The Boo reutrned home that evening, Mrs. Courvoisie was in the kitchen cutting up celery and pickles to mix with the gallon of potato salad she was preparing for her family. Her husband walked in the kitchen, opened a beer, and sat brooding by the kitchen table. In the course of discussing the day's events, The Boo told his wife, who keeps the financial records of the household, to write off thirty dollars for charity. He then related what had passed between him and Mr. Bison. The Boo sympathized with the boy; he had dealt with cadets before who had been crippled by the effects of poverty. These boys were hard and hungry, bargains were made with suckers who did not understand the language of the streets, who could not interpret the world on the other side of the tracks. Mrs. Courvoisie duly recorded the thirty dollar deduction in their budget account. The incident soon passed from memory.

Two years later, the Colonel received a letter from Mr. Bison postmarked in Colorado. It was the first word he had heard. No one seemed to know what had happened after he left The Citadel. The letter was optimistic in tone. Mr. Bison reported that he was playing football for a college in Colorado. He was back on scholarship and was very enthusiastic about his prospects of becoming a starter the following season. One part of his letter was especially poignant.

"Thanks for your help, Colonel. I really appreciated it. Thanks for having faith in me. I'm going to do all right, Colonel. I'm going to do all right."

This letter became the only written communication The Boo ever received from Mr. Bison. Once again the incident of the gas can and the siphon hose and the boy with the oversized neck faded in the daily tedium of the Commandant's Office. These were the years when The Boo's office moved from Bond Hall to Jenkins Hall and The Citadel changed leaders when Hugh P. Harris assumed the reins of leadership from Mark Clark. The case of Mr. Bison was considered closed.

In 1967 Colonel Courvoisie walked from LeTellier Hall in time to see a blue sports car pull up near the parade ground. Someone dressed in a green suit yelled, "Hey, Colonel."

The Colonel answered, "Hello, Mr. Bison. It's good to see you."

"Colonel, I graduated from college, got married, and we are expecting a child."

"That's damn good, Bubba," The Boo answered, smiling.

"I also got a great job. Even thinking about

going back to graduate school for a master's degree."

"They wouldn't take a Bum like you, Bubba," the Colonel laughed.

"Sure they would. By the way, Colonel, I can pay you back the money I owe you."

"You don't have to do that, Mr. Bison, wait till you get settled down and can afford it."

"I would have paid you two years ago, Colonel, but I wanted to give it to you myself." then Mr. Bison paused and wrote a check for thirty-five dollars.

"You only owe me thirty dollars, Bubba."

"That's interest, Colonel. Just interest."

The Groundhogs

A tactical officer, making a routine sweep of "T" Company in the fall of 1963, pulled four cadets for sloppy desks, two cadets for unmade beds, and several others for minor infractions which he usually encounterd on such forays into cadet quarters. But on this particular Wednesday, he found something else which caught his immediate attention. Lying face down on a desk in the second alcove was a photograph of eight cadets. Normally, this would not cause great concern. But something was amiss in the photograph. Two of the cadets, Tony Raffo and Bill Archer, held a shovel while the others were tightly packed into a small, subterranean chamber. A light bulb hung from the ceiling. Unable to piece the mystery together, the Tac brought the photograph to The Boo. Was this picture taken at a beach house? A cadet's home? Rafters were clearly visible. But nothing indicated where the photograph was taken. The Boo did nothing until the Christmas holidays.

Acting on a hunch, he entered 4th Battalion on the first day of furlough. He walked in to the first division alcove. The first press he moved revealed a trapdoor leading under the barracks. He went down the hole and discovered one of the most intricate of cadet projects he ever encountered. The height between the floor of the barracks and the ground was normally three feet. The cadets had removed enough earth so that a man of over six feet could easily stand and move around the room. A television lounge, replete with chairs and sofas, was a prominent feature of the room. A makeshift barber shop decorated one corner and a darkroom for developing photographs graced another. A passageway twenty to thirty feet long dug with care and patience led to a grate by the parking lot. A string of Christmas lights illuminated the entire escape route. Not only did "T" Company seniors have access to the best television had to offer and the finest in black market hair fashioning, they also had a foolproof exit from the barracks whenever they wished. The darkroom proved to be the downfall of the project. One of the photographs developed there was casually left on someone's desk and just as casually confiscated by the Tac. Another photograph showed a cadet named Arthur Douglas on a chair, smiling manfully, and wearing a sweat shirt with the motto, "U.S. Army Sucks," neatly stenciled on it. The wrath of General Clark, usually reserved for acts of God or congress or heresies committed against the Army, descended upon the head of young Arthur, who had the fortune or misfortune, however you look at it, of possessing an Army contract. Clark also had General Garges, the Staff Engineer, solder up the grates and this, in theory, ended the nocturnal expeditions of Tango's seniors.

The Ark

"The Ark" occupies a place of undeniable distinction in the mythology of The Citadel and the cadets. It was the outpost, the mecca of the pot-bellied beer swillers who gazed out of the bars and gates toward the smoking horizon of Charleston. It was the oasis at the end of the tracks; a small, unpretentious bar where the click of billiard balls and the talk of gravel-throated bartenders lured many cadets from the boredom and rigors of evening study period. The Ark caused many cadets to run the gauntlet of the campus guards, the Cadet O.G., and The Boo. A cadet who has never been to The Ark is a Spaniard who has never been to the bull ring. The cadet who has never whispered "screw it" to himself, thrown his books shut in disgust, and ventured into the night in search of cold beer, is the cadet whose spirit has died. The joy of peering out of the bushes by Hampton Park, waiting for the headlights of an unidentified car to leave him in darkness again, never left the cadet. The fugitive then followed the railroad tracks, making sure he left the tracks quickly if the 8:38, Savannah-bound, roared by him. He breathed quickly, his heart pumped several times faster, and he felt like a criminal for doing something considered by most people to be the birthright of every man. He passed the massive shadow of the old baseball park, crossed the street to the Ark, took one more furtive glance around to cover himself, then walked in and shouted to Louie to fix him a "cool one." Louie would mutter some obscenity about the football team and the rest of his night would be spent composing classic defenses of Red Parker's abilities as a coach or whether Vince Petno would try to make it in the Pros.

Psychologically, The Ark was important. It was always there. A place to go if the tension and frustrations proved unbearable, and an illegal beer at The Ark was the nearest a cadet could come to feeding on honeydew or tasting the milk of paradise. He could brag about the forbidden beer for months, cashing in on its status value among other cadets. Each cadet could embellish his own particular story and exaggerate it with his own details. Cadets who spent their whole lives not being noticed won instant notoriety when they announced to their peers, "I went to The Ark last night during Evening Study Period." Magic words were these and for a few moments colorless cadets proudly rose from the smokey depths of oblivion to relate their escape to The Ark, their narrow brushes with The Boo, and their satisfaction at quaffing a cold beer poured with love and care by the strong-veined hand of Louie, the Lip. Cadets said they went to The Ark even if they didn't. Going to The Ark and not getting caught constituted status. But going to The Ark and getting caught was more like ecstasy. There was a certain nobility about a senior private walking tours with stoical resignation as sophomores huddled in whispering aggregates above him, saying, "He got caught going to The Ark." It was like saying, "He was sent to prison for shooting a man who insulted his mother." It was not a disgrace, rather, it was a badge of honor. The Ark stands as a monument to hundreds of cadets who retreated there as a place to enervate waning spirits or a haven of peace in a world of strange juxtapositions. Louie served beer and potato chips to Citadel fugitives for many years. The fugitives came out of the night, some of them reckless, some of them depressed, others lonely, and others just bored. But all of them came to The Ark to forget momentarily the walls and gates. The Ark lives as a symbol that the urge for freedom is often a stronger force than any set of rules.

The Boo knew about The Ark. Everyone did. But he never placed it off limits while he was Assistant Commandant at The Citadel. The cadets were going to find a place to sneak off campus to drink, so he reasoned it was much better to have the place near the campus instead of some disreputable dive further in the depths of Charleston. Boo never had The Ark staked out, never checked it for cadets at regular or irregular intervals, and never tried to break cadets of the habit of sneaking down the railroad tracks for a quick beer. Understanding the cadet psyche well, he knew that certain cadets would leave campus to drink a beer even if they had to drive to the Smoky Mountains to do it. The cadets he caught were caught accidentally, without planning, and without effort.

One night, The Boo and Mrs. Courvoisie were returning to The Citadel campus after visiting a cadet at the Naval Hospital when The Boo spotted two shadows creeping down the railroad tracks near Hampton Park. He jolted the Comet to a stop, leapt out of the car, and boomed out in his death-angel voice, "Come here, Bums."

Had the cadets run for it, churned their legs piston-like and fled into the darkness, The Boo would never have caught them. But like many cadets, the mystique of his voice, and the very power of it, froze them to the spot. Instead of running, they walked meekly over to the green Comet. The Boo took their names, grinned and joked with them, then told them to go enjoy their beer. It would be the last one they would taste for a long time.

On one other occasion, The Boo stumbled upon a group of cadets heading for The Ark. He had taken his wife for a bowl of okra soup and a glass of Michelob beer at Jimmy Dengate's, a place The Boo often went because Jimmy refused to serve cadets. Driving back to the campus, he saw three cadets coming off the railroad track, heading for The Ark. Boo stopped the car right beside them, leapt out, collared two of them immediately, but could not get the third one, who disappeared into The Ark. The Boo took the names of the two cadets. He looked at one of the names carefully, then he said, "Bubba, didn't I give you 3/60 yesterday afternoon?"

"Yes, Sir, you did."

"Well, Bubba, I've got just one thing to say to you."

"What's that, Colonel?"

"Run, Bubba, run like hell."

With that, the cadets ran. Boo entered The Ark; the third cadet had already exited from a side door.

Incident at Capers Hall

In his first summer as Assistant Commandant when he still lived off campus, The Boo received a frantic phone call from the guard at Lesesne Gate.

"Colonel, I think someone is sneaking around Capers Hall. It's dark, but I swear I saw someone go into the building."

"O.K. Bubba, get five cadets together and I'll be over in ten minutes."

Boo arrived on campus about a quarter after ten. The cadets were assembled around the guardhouse. The guard said no one had left the building. Whoever was inside the building had not escaped. He was sure of this. Colonel Courvoisie stationed cadets at each exit of the building. He then selected the largest and most powerful looking cadet in the group to accompany him in a room to room search of the building. Before they entered the front door, they armed themselves with makeshift clubs that could brain a small water buffalo if the occasion arose. Starting with the bottom floor they searched each classroom. They turned on every light as they passed. They worked slowly and methodically, making sure they left no corner unchecked. Boo then walked to the west stairs while Cadet Boney waited at the east stair. On each floor they checked the elevator to make sure no one had used it. First floor, second floor, third floor. Every room, closet,

latrine, and office came under careful scrutiny.
Pressure mounted as The Boo climbed in darkness to the fourth floor. He grasped his club
more tightly. The building was silent and
stoical. When Boo and Cadet Boney flicked on
the hall light, they heard a faint shuffling sound
coming from a small broom closet. Both of
them froze. The Boo said, "Raise that stick,
Bubba." They raised their clubs over their
heads. The quarry, whoever he was, cowered in
darkness. The Boo slipped to the door, opened it
quickly, and stepped back just as quickly. A
shaft of light filled the closet. A thin, cramped
figure stood amidst a phalanx of mops, his head
buried in the mop strings. He was trembling.
Courvoisie ordered him out of the closet. The
two clubs were still in the air. The boy stepped
out with his hands raised in the air. He offered
no resistance at all. The clubs gradually came
down.

Under investigation, the cadet admitted he
broke into Capers Hall to steal exams for the
purpose of selling them in the barracks. He was
a six foot six basketball player who reportedly
had great potential as an athlete. This potential,
however, was never realized at The Citadel.

ERW's

ERW's reveal as much about the nature of The Citadel and her cadets as the Dead Sea Scrolls reveal about the ancient Jewish sect of Essenes. Explaining the function of an ERW to a non-Citadelian is almost as difficult as translating those same scrolls. In military language, this "explanation required written" is a rather unsubtle method of extracting confessions from men who otherwise would remain silent and unpunished. If, for instance, a cadet is absent from a formation, he is asked to write an ERW to explain his whereabouts at the time of this formation. He may have been dying of cholera in the rear of the gymnasium. Therefore, his punishment would not be as severe as it normally would be. The cadet might have been absent because he slept through formation, received a phone call from his girl friend telling him about their blessed event, or any of a thousand reasons. No matter what the reason, the cadet had to explain his absence to the Commandant's Department. It was up to Colonel Courvoisie to read the ERW's and to decide what punishment would be levied on the offender. Most of the time these ERW's were dull documents, sterile as test tubes, without life or personality. They were written in the designated formula; terse, factual, declarative sentences whose primary function was to inform, not to entertain. But the presence of The

Boo—the impalpable, pervasive presence—which somehow invited experiment and stimulated creativity, touched a large segment of the cadet population. As Assistant Commandant he collected a large portfolio of ERW's that surpassed the general level of the genre. He kept the ones that amused him; he saved the ones that by the cold precision of their logic pointed out the inconsistencies in the system. The ERW's you will read on the next pages are a small part of the legacy of ten years in the Commandant's Department. You will note that The Citadel has produced no major poets. You might find grammatical errors, misspellings, and butchered usage. Because of this, The Boo never critized the English Department when they lowered the boom on incoming freshmen. He saw daily the need for improved communication but he also saw the tremendous potential in the cadets. Their humor and unflagging spirit daily entertained him in his office. Not many cadets summoned the nerve to write him flippant, sarcastic ERW's, but those who did never regretted it. He would call them on the phone, chew them out, give them hell and hang up. According to custom, they would worship him from that moment onward.

These ERW's are the stuff of The Citadel, for they capture the bright spirits which dwelt beneath the cover of grey uniforms. They convey the important message that the cadet was ruled by his environment externally only, that The Citadel could control the surface, but not the soul of him beneath it. The ERW's on the following pages are some of the best produced in the eight year Courvoisie reign. The non-

Citadelian will struggle to see humor in any of them; The Citadel graduate will find this chapter the most humorous and memorable in the book.

The ERW, like Gaul, was divided into three parts: the first part stated whether the report was correct or incorrect; the second part gave the specific details surrounding the report; the third part stated whether the offense was intentional, unintentional, or no offense at all. It is all part of the general confusion surrounding life in the barracks. All part of the game.

★

5 March 1964

SUBJECT: Explanation of Report: "Late
                  Division Inspection 1 March,"
                  D/L 4 March

TO: The Commandant of Cadets

1. The report is correct.

2. Due to delicate, amorous circumstances I could not tear myself away from my paramour, and the consequences find me writing this ERW as I was tearfully, regretfully late.

3. The offense was unintentional as I had no control of my emotions.

★

29 February 1965

SUBJECT: Explanation of Report: "Failure to
                  sign out week-end Leave, 2/19/65"
                  D/L 2/26/65

TO: The Commandant of Cadets

1. The report is sadly correct.

2. Due to my frenzied attempt to spit shine my shoes and blitz out a few minor scratches in my brass and still get to my destination on time, the signing out procedure that I would surely have conformed to had I not been so particular about my customarily immaculate appearance, slipped my over-burdened mind. I offer my humble apologies in lieu of any punishment.

3. The offense was very, very unintentional.

★

20 October 1964

SUBJECT: Explanation of Report: "SMI Pet in room 10 October," D/L 19 October

TO: The Commandant of Cadets

1. The report is correct.

2. When I first came upon the cat, she was cold, starving, and did not even purr. Due to the love and affection in my heart, my soul told me to help this orhapn so she could once again purr. Also realizing the family of rats which inhabit my dwelling every night, the cat would be able to help me get rid of the rats. Cat (as I called her) became efficient at exterminating the unwanted creatures. Cat brought joy and comfort to my heart in hearing her once again purr, and in showing her affection for me.

3. The offense was intentional.

(handwritten by The Boo): Your love and devotion should be devoted to higher vertebrates.

★

14 March 1966

SUBJECT: Explanation of Report: "Showing
                     rear end in public 12 March 1966,"
                     D/L 14 March 1966.
TO: The Commandant of Cadets.

1. The report is correct.

2. I was performing a gymnastic clown routine at the halftime of the Blue-White Football
game at Johnson Hagood Stadium, when due to
excessive stretching and bending, the seam in
the rear of my shorts tore. At the time I did not
realize my shorts had torn to the extent which
they had. If I had realized such I would have
confined my movements to eliminate such
undue embarrassment. I was performing the
act as a favor to Mr. Reed of the Athletic
Department, and had no intention of including
such an exhibit in the show. The accident was
an event which could not have been prevented.

3. The offense was not intentional.

★

17 April 1964

SUBJECT: Explanation of Report: "SMI
                     Termite in Pom-Pom 4 April 1964,"
                     D/L 15 April 1964.
TO: The Commandant of Cadets

1. The report is believed to be incorrect.

2. When I fell in for Friday Afternoon
Inspection on the date of the offense, my
uniform (to include the pom-pom on my shako),
was clean and free of extraneous matter, animal
or otherwise. That afternoon, I could not help

but notice the unusually large number of flying insects flitting about my head, harassing me and practically every other man present and standing in formation. This type of insect is called scientifically, Insecta, Arthropoda, Diptera, and is commonly referred to as, the "gnat." During the time between assembly for inspection and the moment the inspecting officer confronted me, a number of some type of insect apparently became enmeshed in the fuzz of my pom pom and were unable to free themselves. Upon falling out after completion of inspection, I checked my shako and found that there were one or two Insecta Arthropoda Diptera ("gnats") imbedded in my pom-pom. They were definitely not, as stated in the report, Insecta Arthropoda Isoptera Reticulitermes, common "termites." Only a small percentage (queens and their mates) are able to fly, and since the ordinary workers and soldiers far outnumber the queens and their mates, and also since the latter types seldom leave the colony, it would have had to have been workers or soldiers that alighted on my pom-pom; and since this type of "termite" is unable to fly, they would have encountered considerable difficulty in reaching my pom-pom between assembly and inspection. The insects on my pom-pom were, therefore, "gnats," rather than "termites." The following visual aids are submitted:

Insecta Arthropoda Isoptera Reticulitermes
"termite"
Insecta Arthropoda Diptera
"gnat"
3. There was no offense.

★

10 May 1966

SUBJECT: Explanation of Report: "Absent
            Pub. Admin. 3 May, D/L 9 May
            1966.
TO: The Commandant of Cadets

My Mother wants me Home! (3/5 or nothing,
PLEASE*)*

1. The report is correct.

2. I was in the placement of office consulting
with Mrs. Renyolds concerning employment
after graduation.

3. The offense was *unintentional*.

CLEMSON WANTS ME!

(rubberstamped by The Boo): **DROP DEAD.** The
punishment he levied: 5/10.

★

8 May 1966

SUBJECT: Explanation of Report: "Blue
            T Shirt 29 April," D/L 6 May
TO: The Commandant of Cadets

1. The report is correct.

2. In my four years at The Citadel, I have
bought innumerable T shirts, all white.
However, due to the pilfering and mangling of
my shirts at the laundry, my supply has
dwindled. Alas, I have sunk to the depths of
poverty in being forced to wear a Citadel
athletic blue T shirt. It seemed, better at the
time, to wear it than the v necked, no necked, no
sided, and no bottomed pieces of cloth, rags,
that I get back from the laundry.

3. The offense was unintentional.

★

2 April 1965

SUBJECT: Explanation of Report: "Absent
Reveille 29 March, D/L 31 March.

TO: The Commandant of Cadets

1. The report is correct.

2. On the 26th of March 1965 at 1700 I departed The Citadel en route to Washington, D.C. on Special Leave. My leave was to terminate on the 28th of March at 2330 hours. My means of travel to my destination was via Air Force C-119. My return trip was to be by commercial airline scheduled to arrive in Charleston at 2200 March 28. I boarded the plane in Washington and it departed on schedule. Upon arriving in the Charleston area the plane, crew and passengers found Charleston enveloped in a blanket of fog 400 feet thick. This is below the commercial airlines minimum requirements for safe landings so the pilot was directed to divert to Jacksonville, Florida. Realizing at the moment of announcement of the diversion that this would cause me to be late returning from leave, I went immediately to the stewardess and asked what could be done to put me on the ground prior to 2330. She assured me that there was no possible way. At this time I requested that the pilot fly near the area of The Citadel campus and I would parachute down and thereby arrive on time. This plan was thwarted when the discovery was made that no parachutes were on board. Returning to my seat I determined to contact the appropriate personnel immediately upon my arrival in Jacksonville and notify them

of my situation. We had not flown more than an hour toward our destination, when we were directed to divert to Orlando, Florida, as the fog conditions existed in Jacksonville. Upon approaching our second alternate objective we were again notified that we would not be able to land due to unfavorable visibility. At this point we began to fear for our gasoline supply but we were assured by the pilot that there remained enough fuel to reach Charlotte, North Carolina, which was reported to be clear of the fog at the time. After some time we arrived in Charlotte and were able to land on the second attempt. The reason for two attempts was because the fog was fast closing in on the Charlotte airfield. Upon entering the terminal I went at once to a telephone and contacted the Officer in Charge at The Citadel. Reporting my situation to him as best I could in three minutes, I received his assurance that the required arrangements would be made for my absence from the campus. Returning to the Eastern Airline desk I found that I was to be housed and fed in a nearby motel at the expense of Eastern Airline and that I would be sent on to Charleston at the first opportunity. The first flight to Charleston left Charlotte at 1250 March 29, 1965, and arrived Charleston at 1345 hours that same day. I reported in to Law Barracks guardroom at approximately 1430 hours March 29, 1965. It was for the above stated series of occurrences that I was absent reveille, the 29th of March.

   3. The offense was unintentional.

★

28 April 1963

SUBJECT: Explanation of Report:
           "Intentionally late class 24 April,"
           D/L 26 April
TO: The Commandant of Cadets

1. The report is correct.

2. Just as Mr. Johnson and I were stepping out of the sallyport at exactly 0800 hours we glanced toward the corner of Bond Hall and Number Four Barracks; there we saw Colonel Courvoisie standing by the mailbox, taking the names of all the cadets who passed him. As an almost involuntary reflex action, we ducked back in the sallyport to make an estimate of the situation. We realized that if Colonel Courvoisie caught us being late to class, he'd give us 5 demerits for this offense, which normally calls for 2. Both of us had gotten 5 demerits from the Colonel for this very thing a few days before, and another 5 would have brought us up to 10, dangerously close to the cut off point. On the other hand, if we could have made it to class without the Colonel seeing us, the section marcher would have reported us late and we would have gotten the usual 2 demerits. At this time, Colonel Courvoisie started walking toward the sallyport; we retreated to the janitor's room, hoping that he would walk past the sallyport and on to the hospital. Unfortunately, the Colonel walked into the barracks looking for us and a few others who had gone too far to give ourselves up and come out of this thing relatively unscathed, so we stood there hiding behind the door in the

janitor's room, hoping we would be able to slip past the Colonel and make it to class before we were ten minutes late, but with the feeling that we didn't stand a chance to escape. We were right; Colonel Courvoisie walked right in the janitor's room, found us, chewed us out, took our names, and booted us out of there. The whole thing was like stepping in quicksand—once we took the initial step, we couldn't stop sinking.

3. The offense was intentional.

★

14 November 1963

SUBJECT: Explanation of Report: "Repeated Tardiness 5 November," D/L 12

TO: The Commandant of Cadets

1. The report is correct.

2. For the most part my tardiness took place during the first month of classes, from 12 September to 10 October. During this period of time I was afflicted with a frequent and almost overwhelming desire for sleep, especially in the mornings from after breakfast until 0800. Although I rarely succumbed to the temptation of the rack in these mornings, my struggles to resist the rack resulted in my acting with an unavoidable lack of haste. Consequently, when class call sounded I was often faced with the problem of deciding to either shave and be late to class or not to shave and be grossly on time. I always chose the former, and subsequently I was reported late to a preponderance of 0800 classes.

Retrospection leads me to the conclusion that

the narcoleptic-like malady with which I was afflicted during the first month of school, with its inherent symptom of repeated tardiness, was a hangover from the habits I formed while attending summer school. It may be remembered that my tardiness in summer school has resulted in my being placed on Colonel Byrd's list of the Top Ten Most Wanted Cadets. Realizing that this inglorious distinction in the Corps of Cadets can only lead to disastrous things, I have taken corrective action in order to improve my status. I have been reported late to only one class since 10 October. This class was not an 0800 class; as a matter of fact, it was an 1100 class to which I was on time. Unfortunately, I had a test in that class for which I had made little or no preparation. Instead of immediately entering the classroom, I lingered in the hall for a few minutes in order to pursue my notes; I got an 80 on the test, and a bonus of 10 demerits for being late. Again, retrospection has shown me that an 80 is not worth 10 demerits. It shall not occur again. I shall repent.

3. The offenses were unintentional.

★

23 September 1962

SUBJECT: Explanation of Report:
           "Officer of the Guard allowing
           ghost in barracks 17 September,"
           D/L 21 September

TO: The Commandant of Cadets

1. The report is believed to be correct.
2. On the evening of Monday, 17 September

1962 at approximately 2330 hours, the Officer in Charge and the Junior Officer of the Day appeared at the front gate of Andrew B. Murray Barracks. While serving in the capacity of Officer of the Guard, I allowed them to enter the barracks. Upon proceeding to check late lights we were confronted with what appeared to be a ghost. Enrobed in a costume resembling an alb it minced backward towards the Bravo Company stairwell. As we approached the unsavory creature, it ascended the stairwell in such a manner that we were unable to continue our pursuit. The Officer in Charge and the Junior Officer of the Day then left the barracks. After the said incident the specter did not reappear.

In regard to the report one should examine more closely the psychic phenomena concerned. Men have not merely believed in ghosts, from the most ancient of days, but have claimed to have seen them. But are there really any ghosts? William James, the great American psychologist, was enthralled by the problem, but never reached any positive conclusion. The noted magician and escape artist, Harry Houdini, carried out a similar crusade up to the end of his life. The findings of various Societies for Psychical Research have never achieved any wide-spread acceptance either.

In search of the truth to the report, I consulted *The Devil's Dictionary* which stated:

"There is one insuperable obstacle to a belief in ghosts.

"A ghost never comes naked; he appears either in a winding-sheet or "in his habit as he lived." To believe in him, then, is to believe that not only have the dead the power to make themselves visible after there is nothing left of them, but that the same power inheres in textile fabrics."

In the light of this knowledge the apparition could have merely been one of several misplaced sheets suddenly hurled up in a gust of wind at a most untimely moment, since it is common knowledge that linen is often displaced on Monday mornings when the Corps of Cadets air their bedding. Such an incident could have quite possibly occurred on Monday, 17 September 1962.

On the other hand, one usually conceives of a ghost as a disembodied spirit of a dead person, unbound by any restrictions whatsoever. Under such circumstances any mortal would be completely defenseless in trying to keep a ghost out of the barracks, as well as any other place on campus. Such an omnipotent creature could freely come and go through the walls, windows, doors, and gates of the barracks, not to mention the more novel approach of leaping over the fourth division onto the quadrangle.

Deducting, however, from his choice of retreating via the stairwell rather than materializing vertically above the quadrangle and then disappearing, and from various campus rumors, I have come to believe that the said ghost was perhaps no more than a "wolf in 'lamb's' clothing."

3. The offense was unintentional.

★

12 May 1966

SUBJECT: Explanation of Report:
            "Weekend leave with confinement,
            6 May 1966" D/L 11 May 1966
TO: The Commandant of Cadets

1. The report is correct.

2. I got the week-end and the confinements and therefore I took the week-end. I thought a week-end took precedent over confinements. *Please Colonel.*

3. The report and offense was completely unintentional.

★

12 March 1964

SUBJECT: Explanation of Report: "Two
            minutes late returning General
            Leave," D/L 11 March
TO: The Commandant of Cadets

1. The report is correct.

2. While being called by one of man's most inborn instincts, that of being loved, the hour of doom when all Boo-fearing cadets turn into pumpkins began its evil approach sooner than I had scheduled my evening to be completed. Realizing my liberty was in jeopardy, I quickly (but quite efficiently) concluded my affair and with all due godspeed, my fair damsel clinging to my neck, took leave of her most hospitable abode and made for my chariot. Alas and alack, my chariot would not start, for the death of its prized battery, overworked and sternly overlooked in the annual chariot check at The Fortress.

Push as she did, (for I deigned to soil my proud uniform), my lass could not conjure the strength to attain the proper speed. "Oh, woe is me," thought I, but low and behold to my aid in that moment of crisis came her chivalrous and valorous father, and with a push from his wife's mighty back (for he, too, deigned to soil his proud uniform) started yon chariot, and with a final kiss from my fair damsel off went I into the gloom of the night only to enter The Fortress gates into the understanding and benevolent arms of the Officer in Charge, alas, two blissful minutes late.

For my fate ˉ now wait in dire anxiety and surely no matter what my sanction, I shall fiercely face my penalty.

3. The offense was unintentional.

★

23 March 1964

SUBJECT: Explanation of Report:
            "Talking at parade," D/L
            21 March 1964
TO: The Commandant of Cadets

1. The report is correct, I think.

2. Hardly does a parade pass each week that I don't have something to say at one time or another. However, I'm sure that the date of the infraction in question is the parade which was held on March 13th which was the first day of Corps Day Weekend. I will not attempt to deny that I sinned, however, I'm sure that my comment was only said at a whisper and it could not have been heard by all the parents and guests who were attending this function. It

is hard to refrain from saying something at a parade at which many of our beloved ones are watching. Nevertheless, since this parade was in celebration of our 121st birthday and since this was the parade at which I sinned, I please ask for a birthday present in this case, i.e., no demerits.

3. The offense was unintentional, but the talking was intentional.

★

27 November 1963

SUBJECT: Explanation of Report: "Unauthorized persons in barracks
16 November," D/L 26

TO: The Commandant of Cadets

1. The report is correct.

2. On the weekend of the offense I was amazed to receive a surprise visit from two friends which I had made at summer camp. They had driven to The Citadel all the way from Connecticut in order to witness with their own eyes the wonder of The Citadel. Being tired, confused, and innocent of the ways of the big city of Charleston, I could not turn them loose into the claws of Charleston. Furthermore, being young Second Lieutenants on their way to branch school, they had no money to spare. Thus it was in the finest tradition of The Citadel that I exhibited The Citadel Code (page 78, 1963 Guidon).

"... to exhibit good manners on all occasions,"

and

". . . to be generous and helpful to others
and to endeavor to refrain them from
wrong doing."

If I had turned them out into the cold, cruel,
bitter night of Charleston, who knows what
"wrong-doings" and vices their pure hearts
would have been subjected to.

3. Thus it was purely an unselfish act which I
committed, upheld in the finest tradition of The
Citadel, for their safety, and for the good name
of this school.

4. The offense was intentional.

★

19 May 1966

SUBJECT: Explanation of Report:
           "Improper D.I., 14 May
           1966," D/L 18 May 1966
TO: The Commandant of Cadets

1. The report is correct.

2. One of my men (your lambs) was on a
weekend leave, and was reported present by an
accident of Cadet W.R.S. Curtis (18878). Having
noted his sins Cadet Curtis has enrolled in
Clemson.

3. The offense was sinful but forgivable.

★

18 May 1966

SUBJECT: Explanation of Report: "Failure
           to sign restrictions 13 May,"
           D/L 16 May.
TO: The Commandant of Cadets

1. The report is correct.

2. I dare to say on 13 May,
   I was in my room there to stay.
   But, "Von Ryan's Express" was on at the
       flic,
   So, in that room I could not stick.
   The temptation was such an affliction,
   And lo, I forgot my restriction.
   The show was what one could expect,
   And was over at 9:30 as I reflect.
   On my way back to the barrcks dim,
   Some varmint stopped me before I went in.
   And in her car we frolicked till midnight,
   So this explains my present plight.
3. The offense was unintentional.

★

SUBJECT: Reconsideration of Awards,
                "Old Lady 02/26/65,"
                D/L 5 March 1965
TO: The Commandant of Cadets

1. The report is believed to be in extreme
doubt.
2. The question posed is now about
   (Oh that one could ever doubt)
   The sex of one so young and strong
   A lad who stays away from wrong.

   Twas on a morning bleak and cold
   I started for classes with heart so bold
   I fought the urge to head back to bed
   By pulling my scarf over my head.

   "Hey, Old Lady," came the cry
   And to one as virile as I

The verdict could only one way go
A strong, emphatic, definite No!

★

28 April 1965

SUBJECT: Reconsideration of Award:
"No name tags in trousers turned into tailor shop 21 April," D/L April 25.

TO: The Commandant of Cadets

1. The report is believed to be incorrect.

2. The trousers in question were turned into the tailor shop with name tags sewn in their proper place. These name tags have been in the trousers since they were issued to me in my freshman and sophomore years. However, during the current school year my name has been legally changed; and when compared to the vast amounts of proverbial red tape which had to be processed in order that this fine institution be cognizant of the fact that I have remained one in the same person, the changing of the name on the name tags on the inside of the fly of my dress and full dress trousers seemed quite insignificant. When these trousers were placed in the custody of the tailor shop for summer storage and repair, it was brought to my attention that great difficulty would be encountered by the tailor shop staff and that the system used to process all the many thousands of garments would be reduced to utter chaos. Upon talking this problem over with the individuals immediately concerned, it was agreed that a simple and effortless solution was at hand. All that was necessary was for me

to order at the cadet store a quantity of cloth name tags and which when arrived would be brought to the tailor shop and the new name tags would replace the old. The name tags have been ordered and no more complications to this minor problem have occurred. At the present time there is a feeling of complete understanding and cooperation between the staff at the tailor shop and myself. I fully understand that in the military way of life there exists a system of rewards and punishments. I also understand that punishments are awarded to reprimand sub-standard performance and offenses against established rules and regulations. In this particular incident I fail to see any offense or performance which might be rated as being below par.

3. There is believed to be no offense.

★

22 April 1965

SUBJECT: Explanation of Report: "Abs 090 Accty 304 Test 9 April 1965," D/L 21 April 1965.

TO: The Commandant of Cadets

1. The report is correct.
2. Alas, General Patton had his troubles, and so do I,

    But when I discovered my mistake, I was so embarrassed I could die.

    A small military blunder for Patton is for me a colossal mistake.

    Patton would simply dismiss it, but I have to shake and wait.

    Out of the drudgery of everyday routine, I

had my days mixed up and thought it was one day when indeed it was another.

I have sinned through thoughtless memory and I am now to be judged, so, I can only beg for mercy and ask you that in my situation,

"What would Patton have done?"

3. The offense was unintentional.

★

23 March 1964

SUBJECT: Explanation of Reports:
           "Absent Steel Design 0900
           26 April, Absent Concrete 1100 26
           April,"
           D/L 10 May.
TO: The Commandant of Cadets

1. The reports are correct

2. For about three days previous to this, I had been having nightmares and was unable to sleep. On the morning of the offense I started having hallucinations while I was awake. Whenever I would sit down or lay down, I would start seeing things which I knew weren't there. I went to class and while waiting for it to start, I kept having the same trouble. I had the feeling that I was going to start screaming and had a hard time controlling my temper with anyone who came near me. I left LeTellier Hall and walk around in the rain for several hours trying not to think about anything although I was fully conscious of the fact that I should have been in class and was going to be reported for not going.

3. The offenses were intentional.

★

SUBJECT: Explanation of Report: "Smoking
                   on Campus Second Offense
                   8 December," D/L 17 December
TO: The Commandant of Cadets

1. The report is correct.

2. As I was having a nicotine fit at the time, I did not wish to leave my cigarette behind in the messhall only half-finished, but at the same time my presence was required in a class which I had. Since my route back to barracks was an inconspicuous one, no outsider saw me smoking, which was in accordance with the reason the no-smoking rule was made. Incidentally, I field-stripped the cigarette and retained the paper so that it would not mar the truly striking beauty of our campus, which was in accordance with another reason for the no-smoking rule.

3. The offense was intentional.

★

                                        19 October 1964

SUBJECT: Explanation of Report:
                   "SMI Pet in Room 10 October,"
                   D/L 19 October
TO: The Commandant of Cadets

1. The report is correct

2. In the interest of and for the promotion of science, a member of the;

Kingdom Animal
      Phylum Chordata

Group Vertebrata
  Subphylum Gnathostomata
   Super Class Tetrapoda
    Infraclass Eutheria
     Order Carnivora
      Suborder Fissipedia
       Family Felidae
        Genus Felis
         Species domestica

commonly known as the domestic cat was invited to make her humble abode in room 2202 where she was discovered and "deported" immediately with the immediate consequence being an "H" on the D/L for the industrious, well-meaning scientist. The main purpose for the invitation was to make an intensive study of her external features with special emphasis centered upon the depression and contraction of her muscles. It was hoped by the scientist that this work would stand him in good stead when the external features of the cat were studied by him next semester in comparative anatomy.

3. The offense was intentional.

(handwritten by The Boo): Sad Too Bad Not The Fad   3/5

★

SUBJECT: Explanation of Circumstances: "Appearing at an unexpected hour, at an unauthorized dwelling, without written permission, or an oral invitation," May 17, 1962

TO: The Commandant of Cadets

1. The report is correct.

2. Sir, it is with much respect and humble gratitude that I appear before you in this manner tonight. My story is a sad one, and it is written with tears in my eyes. The truth is, Sir, I am a poor, ugly orphan child with feet that resemble a chicken's. For four long years I have lived here at The Citadel in shame and utter humiliation. For you see, Sir, I am what you might call an "ugly duckling" or a "gross slob." The few dear friends that I once had, have all turned their backs on me. My parents disowned me when I was old enough to eat porridge with my fingers. With my personal appearance, ghoulish at it is, to go along with my equally warped mind you can easily see, Sir, I need someone to turn to. Since I needed someone to turn to but could not perceive of any one who could be so kind, my friends graciously decided to solve my grave problem. It is at this point that I will stop and offer thanks to you and your family for taking me into your humble dwelling. If I should cry in the middle of the night, don't worry, don't panic, just wash my skoady feet and feed me some warm milk and cookies. I don't need to be burped.

3. The offense was most graciously intentional.

/s/Bobbie
ALIAS "THE TRACKER"
CADET SLOB 1st CLASS
O. G. NUMBER 3 BARRACKS

Mike

Mike O'Brien did not want to come to the Citadel in the first place. He hated the idea of going to a military college. He begged his parents to let him go somewhere else. But his father, a Marine Corps Colonel, thought the discipline and regimented life of The Citadel would be good for his troublesome son. Mike was a free spirit in high school and his father reasoned that the boy needed a period of confinement and control during his college days. In the fall of 1963, Mike entered Lesesne Gate. He entered Lesesne Gate bitterly. From his first day as a plebe, Mike fought the system with unwavering dedication.

He gained notoriety his very first week. In those days only seniors were allowed to walk across the hallowed turf of the parade ground. Mike was caught twice during plebe week sauntering across this forbidden land. In the same week one of his classmates bumped into him during a sweat party and Mike landed a right cross on his jaw. An angular platoon leader was giving Mike a little extra attention one night after mess and was slightly taken aback when Mike called him a "skinny little bastard." Within two weeks, the name "O'Brien" had won a permanent niche in campus conversation. O'Brien stories enlivened bull sessions during Evening Study Period. Seniors from three battalions traveled down to Bravo Company to catch a glimpse of the foolhardy knob who defied the system with such disregard for his own personal comfort. "B" Company upperclassmen devised every torture known to man trying to break O'Brien's spirit. They put him "on the wall" for hours at a time. They stuffed him into a steel locker and blew cigarette smoke into the vents. They made him do pushups until he dropped from exhaustion. They humiliated him at mess, starved him at mess, and refused to acknowledge his presence at mess. They screamed obscenities at him; they appealed to his pride and masculinity. They did all these things, but they never broke O'Brien. He fought The Citadel with every waking breath and with all the resources available to him. No matter how much pressure the upperclassmen exerted against him, nothing seemed to phase O'Brien. When the battalion commander tried to have a serious, man-to-man talk with him, O'Brien laughed in his face. The shocked battalion commander, who was accustomed to being treated like an anthropomorphic god by freshmen, decided to present the case of O'Brien to the Commandant's Department and The Boo.

The Boo gave O'Brien an order for failure to follow verbal commands. On the first day of tour formation The Boo went up to O'Brien and congratulated him heartily for being the first member of his class to walk tours. This was akin to being congratulated for being the first to contract whooping cough. The Boo then asked O'Brien what exactly was eating him, why he could not adapt to the system, and why he had gained such widespread notoriety in a brief two weeks. O'Brien listened to The Boo stoically. He said "Yes, Sir" in the proper places. He was neither disrespectful nor obsequious. But after a five minute conversation, The Boo knew intuitively that O'Brien was trying his damndest to separate himself from the Corps of Cadets.

The Boo moved him to Fourth Battalion in an effort to save him. Had O'Brien been a typical knob, this strategy might have been effective. But O'Brien was a super-knob whose reputation traveled before him, spreading the word of his deeds and exploits before his arrival. When he entered Fourth Battalion, he was a marked man. He was given no chance. The Corps had marked O'Brien for execution. In the harsh law of the Corps, the freshman who completely rebelled against the system was driven out of The Citadel by any means necessary. The hazing of this marked freshman grew more and more severe until the freshman neared the breaking point. He was given individual attention by packs of sergeants and corporals who surrounded him, shouted in his ear, abused him physically and verbally, and terrified him into leaving the school. The Citadel can be a vicious world. What I have described will not be understood by those men who graduated from The Citadel at an earlier period. The Citadel was more refined then. The hazing was not brutal. But after the second world war, a theory circulated around the military men of the college that the tougher the environment, the more resilient and more durable the leader produced. So graduates who sent their sons to The Citadel after the war never fully understood why their sons could not accept a system they had found to be so stimulating to their young manhood. In the early 1960's, the plebe system was a kind of inquisition. When O'Brien came along, General Tucker was effecting changes in the fourth class system which were resented bitterly by the Corps. The changes came too late to make any substantial difference in the fate of Mike O'Brien. O'Brien faced daily harassment by red-faced squad leaders. They stepped on his formation shoes (which is worse than having someone step on your mother's face if you are a freshman). They tried to get his classmates to give him the cold shoulder. Through all of this, O'Brien remained as passive as a cigar store Indian. He arrived at The Citadel physically hard. As time passed, he became harder.

The upperclassmen stuck O'Brien with over fifty demerits the first month of school. He served confinements until, as he put it, "his ass was one big callus." Tour formation always found him with a rifle slung carelessly over his shoulder. Seniors would stop him on his way to class to rack him for some real or imagined offense. The pressure was so intense and his reputation among the Corps so malignant that O'Brien soon had nothing to lose. On one famous occasion, when the upperclassmen pulled a crackdown on the knobs, and all the fury of sergeantdom was released on the heads of the freshmen, several people choked back thoughts of homicide when someone noticed O'Brien laughing in the middle of the sweat party. One sergeant pulled O'Brien out of the shower room and stood him up against the wall. By this time, O'Brien was laughing hysterically.

The upperclassmen momentarily forgot about their party. They sent all the other freshmen to their rooms. O'Brien quit bracing suddenly, tilted his cap over his nose in a rakish angle, leaned against the wall, and lit up a cigarette. The upperclassmen stood aghast, too mad to speak, too surprised to respond in a legitimate manner. O'Brien smoked his cigarette slowly and thoughtfully. Then he looked at a platoon sergeant—an emaciated, spindly platoon sergeant—and said, "Smith, you are so ugly. I bet you never had a date in your life. Look at your body, Smith. My god, son, you have the worst body I have ever seen in my life."

O'Brien took another drag on his cigarette. He then turned to another sergeant and said, "McMillan, you are big crap around this school, but you would be *nothing* in any other school in the country. Wouldn't that be a damn joke. McMillan in a fraternity."

O'Brien did fairly well in his denunciation of the powers above him, until he called the company commander a "fat pig." Then the rulers of Fourth Battalion closed their broken ranks and swarmed all over O'Brien once again. Yet it was one of O'Brien's finer moments as a cadet.

From the initial moment he walked on to The Citadel's campus, O'Brien's one purpose in life was to leave Lesesne Gate as quickly as possible. Demerits piled up on him like ants on a dead grasshopper. The Boo looked at scores of white slips on O'Brien every day. The Boo and the rest of the Commandant's Department knew that O'Brien's days within the Corps were numbered. When The Boo talked to O'Brien, the boy stated that he despised the school, but his father refused to let him leave. Finally in sheer desperation, O'Brien walked out of his room on a Saturday when he was supposed to be serving confinements. The guard tried to stop him, but O'Brien said he was going to watch a tennis match. The guard pulled him for skipping confinements. When O'Brien had to write an ERW explaining his actions, he stated that he was in his room and had served all confinements that day. Seventy cadets saw him at the tennis match. O'Brien won his freedom from The Citadel by committing an intentional honor violation.

The man who stormed into Courvoisie's office the day of O'Brien's resignation was a tall, handsome soldier. He was square-shouldered, well-proportioned, and angry as hell. A silver star hung from his blouse. Colonel O'Brien foamed in repressed anger.

"My name is O'Brien," the Colonel said.

"Courvoisie, Sir," The Boo replied.

"Why does my son have to resign? He's made it this far. Why don't you let him finish the year?"

"Colonel, your son has been in trouble all year long. He's been trying to leave The Citadel ever since he got here."

"Well, why wasn't my wife or I notified about it? We thought Mike was doing well up here."

Colonel Courvoisie challenged. "I have personally sent four letters stating that your son had exceeded the limit of demerits, and asking that you encourage your son to shape up, so he could remain at The Citadel."

"You never sent those letters to my house." Colonel O'Brien replied angrily.

Colonel Courvoisie asked Mrs. Petit to bring in the file on Mike O'Brien. In the file were four letters concerning excess demerits and three letters concerning punishment orders. Colonel O'Brien looked at the letters and mumbled something about the wife "always taking the boy's side."

Courvoisie told Colonel O'Brien that The Citadel is not the right school for every boy. Mike O'Brien left The Citadel that day without a single regret and without looking back.

The Ballad of Andy Latta

Of all the great, muscled jocks who ripple their way southward to wage battle on The Citadel gridiron, none has inspired the number of legends or neared the proportions of an epic hero as Andy Latta. Andy looked like an uprooted oak tree. His muscles were like the knots of a dock rope and his temper was quick and volcanic. Upperclassmen knew instinctively that the Italian boy who stood before them on plebe night could break a human head like a ripe cantaloupe, so they treated him gingerly on that night and all the other nights of his freshman year. One thing almost everyone agreed on the instant he came in sight; Andy was a man.

Like many kids from tough neighborhoods, Andy knew the ins and outs of street fighting and gang warfare well. His gang ruled "the turf" of his home town and much of its success was due to Andy's affinity for smashing the noses and splintering the jaws of rival gang members who ventured into forbidden territory. Football rescued him from the gang. He made the delightful discovery that football was a socially acceptable form of head hunting. So he began to remove limbs, gouge out eyes, and kick out the teeth of any lineman intrepid enough to challenge his charge across the line for the opposing quarterback. His prowess on the football field brought him to The Citadel.

Any boy weaned on the streets with a big city gang is going to have certain basic problems in adjusting to the regimen of Citadel life. Andy thought it stupid to follow every rule of *The Blue Book*, so he refused to adhere to some of them. This brought him in direct contact with The Boo, who ruled the turf around the Commandant's Department. Andy first gained fame the summer between his freshman and sophomore year. He drove in Lesesne Gate one night and decided it was ridiculous to drive all the way around the parade ground. He had learned in physics class that the shortest distance between two points is a straight line. Adhering to this principle, he jumped the curb by the library and drove his car across the parade ground to first battalion. It was not a bad idea except he failed to notice the shadow of The Boo in the sallyport. The Boo ranted at Latta for a good thirty minutes. The legend had started.

Then Andy went on a motorcycle kick. The sight of a Citadel cadet on a motorcycle roaring across the Cooper River Bridge in dress uniform was strange indeed. The cadet image seemed a bit ludicrous when Andy pulled up to a stop light, revved his motor, then sped off to a party at the Isle of Palms. On one occasion he became the talk of the town. Andy took his girl to a Citadel Hop on his motorcycle. He arrived at her house resplendent in his full dress uniform, silk gloves on his hands, and a new shine on his inspection shoes. His girl bounced out of the house wearing a full length formal, blew her tolerant father a kiss, consoled her weeping mother, and climbed up behind Andy.

They zoomed off into the night. Puzzled motorists stared after them. People waved. Some blew their horns. Andy and his girl kept going, oblivious to the ripple they were causing as they passed by. They roared onto The Citadel campus, the big Harley sputtering defiantly. Andy rode up to the door of the armory, offered his arm to his beloved, and marched into the prom like he owned the State of Rhode Island. Some cadets who witnessed the scene felt Andy would make a better member of the Hell's Angels than the Corps of Cadets. Of course, Andy didn't give a damn.

It is important to remember Andy's background. It explains many things about a particular incident in the spring of 1966. On this night, something snapped in Andy. The dark side of Andy Latta was unleashed upon a trembling world. Some atavistic impulse triggered Andy into action and gave The Citadel one of her more memorable nights. It started with a rumor. A group of Charleston hoods had beaten up Rick Clifford, Andy's roommate, while Rick was playing pool at The Ark. The rumor further specified that these were the same hoods who had lead-piped a couple of cadets the summer before and left them bleeding in an uptown alley. Though the rumor was false, Andy did not realize it. In the code of the Gang, each member was a brother. If one brother was beaten, then someone had to pay. He left the barracks on the run. A contingent of "B" Company jocks and weight lifters followed him. They wanted to see the molars fly.

He entered The Ark and looked quickly around. Clifford wasn't there. "They must have hidden the body," Andy said to himself, possibly remembering some cardinal rule of his gang days. Andy spotted a suspicious looking group in the back of the bar, playing pool, and minding their own business. They looked guilty to Andy. Some unfortunate greaser made a spurious remark to Andy. He caught the first fist of the evening. He flew across the pool table and landed under the legs of a pinball machine. The boy spit a tooth out of his bleeding mouth. Meanwhile, Andy had taken on the rest of the pool players. His fists pounded anyone who came into range. No method prevailed in his quixotic annihilation of those who had wronged his roommate. Teeth clattered on the floor. Blood spewed from four noses. The hoods bounced cue balls off Latta's head. They swung cue sticks at his body. This just served to fan his wrath. One foolish lad shouted to Latta that he was nothing but a "Goddamn wop." Andy ran up to him, stuck two fingers between his teeth and cheeks, and ripped as hard as he could. The boy's lips were split open in two places. No other challenger appeared. Nor did anyone else mention Andy's Italian heritage. Satisfied that he had avenged his roommate sufficiently, Andy returned to the barracks. Several days later he received a bill for $173. This was the combined doctor bill of all the boys he mauled at The Ark.

Boo stormed into The Ark the very next day. The story of Latta mopping up half the refuse of Charleston on The Ark's floor dominated conversation around The Citadel. The image of the cadet as scholar, soldier, and gentleman was hard pressed to include the cadet as bar-fighter or hood-pounder. Boo walked up to the owner of The Ark and asked to speak to him.

"I'm Courvoisie of The Citadel. I heard one of my lambs got into a fight here last night. I just wanted to tell you if any cadet ever gets in a fight down here again or if one of my boys gets hurt in any way, I am going to put this place off limits to cadets and post guards around it to make sure nobody comes here. Do you understand me, Sir?"

"Yes, Sir, Colonel." The owner understood perfectly.

Andy Latta graduated with his class. To do this, he curtailed his career as an all-southern conference tackle. He quit football his senior year in order to study. On graduation day he brought Colonel Courvoisie a gift. It was a charcoal portrait of The Boo done by Latta's sister.

"Thanks for everything, Colonel. I wanted to get you something nice, so my sister did this."

"Latta, only God and I know what a bum you really are." Both of them smiled.

The Scowl on Monk's Face

Nobody messed with Monk. This was an unwritten law in the early sixties around the first battalion. Monk was an Irishman; a surly, brusque graduate of an Irish ghetto in the Bronx. When aroused to the full fever-pitch of his anger, Monk was a formidable and dangerous adversary. He smiled infrequently. The few friends he made at The Citadel became aware of a distance in Monk, some impenetrable wall he erected to separate his friends from even the slightest awareness of his past. And it was this same past that provided the clue to the burden and the scowl Monk always dragged with him. For a long time, Monk walked the campus in silence, rebuffed overtures at friendship, projected a dark and irredeemable personality to the world he passed. It took a while, but Monk finally told a few close friends his story.

Monk's grandparents had been driven to America when the great famine decimated the potato crop in Ireland. They made the best of their misfortune. Monk's grandfather prospered in the New World. A ruthless determination and adamant refusal to buckle under to the pressure of competitors had netted the family a considerable fortune. A new noun, millionaire, described Monk's grandfather, and grandpa liked the sound of it. Like many of the Irish patriarchs who immigrated to America in the late nineteenth century, he was fiercely protective and possessive of his children. All of his children followed his directives to the last syllable. All of them married the proper spouses and entered the proper professions. All except one. Monk's mother embarked on a destiny not supervised by the stern visage of her father. She fell in love with a handsome Irish face and strong calloused hands and lips that drank beer from a laborer's bench. She fell in love with a factory worker named Mike. A nice guy without money, without a future, and without the approval or respect of his girl friend's father. They were married.

The full fury of the family was vented against both of them. The girl had committed the unpardonable sin of falling in love without the approval of her father. A family council was held under the auspices of the wronged patriarch. Monk's mother and father were banished from the family circle.

Mike and his family fared poorly. He lost one job after another while his wife suffered under the humiliation and disdain of the family who rejected and ignored her. The family, with collective solidarity, refused to acknowledge the presence of their former member. Cinderella had chosen her impoverished prince and the kingdom she betrayed would never be opened to her again. Mike, possibly because of the grave pressures exerted on him, or because he bore the full responsibility of his wife's exile, turned to the bottle. Poverty of the cruelest kind entered their lives and the lives of their children, who appeared almost yearly at regular intervals.

Monk was the first born child. His formative years were hungry years. The streets served as the training ground for his youth, where the quick fist and the quick foot were the two most important elements of survival. Monk had both. He left a string of bloody noses down the long row of houses on his street and arrived home sporting the same on many occasions.

When he was twelve years old his mother was taken to the hospital. Two days later she was dead. It happened so quickly that her family had no time to make reparations or amends. They had no time to accept her back into the fold with outstretched and forgiving arms. She had died without the courtesy of allowing her family to say they were sorry. The funeral was thick with flowers and voices raised in grief. Monk's father was an outcast, a pariah at the funeral of his own wife. Naturally, the great family decided in a sober-faced council that the children could not continue to live with their father. So Monk and the kids moved from the sinister alleys of the Bronx to the elegant mansions inhabited by New York's most affluent society. Monk suddenly found himself thrust into a world of silk and linen, where no one cursed or wrote on the bathroom walls, where no one fought or bloodied anyone's nose, and where no one put their elbows on the table or sneezed without covering their mouths. He attended a respectable private school, was tutored in etiquette by a lemon-faced aunt, and walked through the corridors of his grandfather's house with the gnawing thought that every step he took was a betrayal of his father. The scowl on Monk's face was becoming pronounced.

He was sent to The Citadel where, it was thought, the discipline and Spartan existence would make him appreciative and grateful for the luxuries his grandfather's house provided. The plebe system barely challenged the boy who had fought in the slums of the Irish tenement sections of New York. His body, hard and sinuous, adapted easily to the rigors of nightly sweat parties and mental harassment. But the plebe system did nothing to alleviate the bitterness which was becoming the key element in the composition of Monk's personality. His classmates were aloof and more than a little wary of the mirthless Irishman. A year passed before Monk came to trust anyone enough to tell them his story. He told it to few people. They were his friends. The words surfaced bitterly.

"Whenever I go home to New York I walk into that goddamn big house and listen to my grandfather tell me what a son of a bitch my father was. I just eat my food and listen without saying anything. The next day I go out looking for my Dad. I go from bar to bar in the places I know he hangs out. Eventually, I find him all dirty and drunk and I say, 'Dad, you want to go out for dinner?' 'Sure, Monk,' he says to me. 'I could sure use a good meal!' I take him up to a hotel room I've rented for him, let him take a good bath, all hot and everything. Then I take him out for a steak dinner. Neither one of us talks much. Just sit there and grin every once in a while. I want to tell him things and I know he wants to tell me things, but mostly we just eat and look at each other or talk about baseball. After the meal, I take him back to the hotel and put him to bed. He drops off to sleep almost immediately. I put a twenty in his pocket. Then I leave. It kills me to know that he's always wandering around. Always wandering around. Never doing nothing. Just moving around all the time."

One of Monk's friends told Colonel Courvoisie the story. The Boo had become friendly with Monk while the latter was walking tours in the second battalion sallyport and had wondered what chip rested so securely on Monk's shoulder. The Boo would gently banter the frowning Irishman as Monk paced back and forth with his rifle on his shoulder. Monk would chide back and the two soon found themselves stopping to chat whenever they met on campus. Boo signed several weekend passes for Monk, and a few other favors cemented a friendship which would last for two years.

It is difficult to describe Boo's relationship to cadets in cases like this. With Monk as with many other cadets, it seems probable that The Boo represented the father-image that Monk so desperately needed: a warm, yet stern figure who was a blend of warmth and strength in equal proportions, and who asked nothing in return for his interest and regard for you. As The Boo has said on occasion, "Many boys are sent to The Citadel because their parents had failed them somewhere along the line. Because the parents realize their failure, they figure that The Citadel can do the job for them. Some of them feel that discipline will compensate for the lack of love. More than our share of kids come from broken homes or from parents who just didn't give a damn."

Monk came to The Boo in his office many times just to talk. The Boo listened and gave advice. They laughed and talked of many things. Monk never told The Boo about his father; Boo never asked Monk to tell him. But he did complain bitterly about his aunt who never let up on him, never relented in her criticism, and never withdrew the pressure she felt was her duty to levy upon him.

During his senior year the pressure became extremely intense. Monk told The Boo that he didn't know how much longer he could take her harping and bitching. The next day the afore-mentioned aunt received a phone call from Lt. Colonel T. N. Courvoisie. "Madame, this is Courvoisie, The Citadel. I just wanted to call and tell you Monk is a good boy. You are put-ting a little too much pressure on him right now. Graduation is coming up and he needs to concentrate on getting out of The Citadel. He can't be thinking about what you're telling him and what his professors are telling him at the same time. So, Madame, I just wanted to call and let you know your nephew is doing fine at The Citadel, but needs to know that you love and support him. If you need anything, please feel free to call me."

The aunt uttered a few respectful "Yes Sirs," but she had not said, "Go to hell," or, "It's none of your business." In the beginning of the book the stentorian voice of The Boo was discussed at length. In person, it can freeze hummingbirds in mid-flight, but on the telephone it is something else indeed, something almost god-like in its power to transfix and to control.

Boo's humanity is expressed in person by gentle modulations of the great voice or a sudden softness of the large, playful eyes. He is almost incapable of gentleness on the telephone. Call him at The Citadel sometimes, and imagine you are Moses talking to the Burning Bush. It is not difficult. Monk's aunt let the pressure off Monk.

Monk did not graduate with his class. He went to summer school to get enough quality points to satisfy The Citadel's requirements for the diploma. He is making the Air Force a career.

Christmas

Each Christmas since 1965 The Boo has sent out three or four hundred copies of his annual Christmas message to his departed lambs. Every cadet who keeps in touch with him receives this Christmas greeting from The Boo. The letter is written in the typical Courvoisie style, without flourish and without pretense of literary merit. Within the letter are the standard Courvoisie jokes, the esoteric pitch of Corps humor, which the uninitiated find boring, but the ex-cadet finds hilarious. The letters are newsy and short. They often mention the more infamous senior privates, five-year men and muscle-headed jocks. They tell of Citadel trends, changes in personnel, and shifts of emphasis within the disciplinary system. In essence, these letters keep many alumni in touch with The Citadel who ordinarily would hear nothing from the school. One cadet who received the Christmas greeting wrote The Boo and told him it was the first time he had heard from The Citadel in eight years. Several ex-cadets have joined the alumni association after reading the letter. Since most alumni who attended the school when the shadow of The Boo covered the campus remember themselves as lambs and bums, the letter is a very personal and intimate reminder of their college days. The school is there. The Boo is alive and well. The Corps is changing; the school is changing, but The Boo is there, thinking long thoughts, and believing in the worth and value of the graduates . . . and the school.

'65

Dear

I can't tell you how happy it makes the old Boo to hear from his former "little lambs." How is the cold cruel world? I bet they don't love you and treat you as kindly as we did.

Now for a little gossip. Summer school went pretty well. I only had to ship two this past year, for stealing and both from well to do families. I am quite proud that our Honor System works in the summer time as they were both turned in by cadets.

We started the year off with 70 more cadets than we had beds, so we were quite crowded. The upperclasses have taken the inconvenience in good grace and we have lost only about 75 cadets as of the Christmas furlough.

As you know the football team did not win many. But I want you to know that you can be proud of them. They fought all the way. The University of South Carolina had to appeal to their team at half time to beat The Citadel for a dying Carolina football player. West Virginia and George Washington were never the same after our cadets hit him. I could name name after name of outstanding cadets on the squad, good in academics, cadet rank and fighting football players, very few bums and they were only minor. Charlie McDonald always needing a haircut and Wilbur Fallow always needing a shoe shine. That Wilbur is one helleva football player.

Our new President, General Harris, is still looking around, not saying much. He gave all of The Corps Thanksgiving leave this year. At his inauguration on 15 October he rescinded all punishment, by the 15 December there were 61 black "little lambs" walking tours, plus over 400 lambs serving confinements.

This year I sat in the senior date section at the football games. Didn't need a drink the fumes kept me going. One cadet introduced a non-Citadel man in Citadel uniform into the senior date section. I was lucky enough to spot him. The cadet only received 10/40/2 months.

The basketball team has only two veterans, but they are fighting.

President Harris is putting complete new beds and furniture in the cadet rooms. In about four years it will be The Hilton Citadel.

My wife has lost 60 pounds. I have lost 40 pounds by dieting. My son, Alfred, has lost 50 pounds by being a plebe in Company A. My daughter will graduate from U.S.C. in June '66 with a degree in Biology (took her three years) and has already been accepted at the Medical College of South Carolina to study to be a real human doctor.

Oh yes, the plebes are the worse class to ever enter The Citadel, but they are being "shaped up" and will make the grade. The class of '66 is doing a good job.

The Citadel has had at least 8 graduates killed in Viet Nam and quite a number wounded. Major Savas, a former Assistant Professor of Military Science, died in Viet Nam in October '65 from a back injury he had before he left here.

We are always proud of our lambs.

My family and I, and Miss Betsy send our love and regards.

                                        Boo

                                        '66

Merry '66 Christmas, Lamb,

As usual we are marching along. September '66 saw over 2,100 cadets, with only 650 "knobs." Most of the remainder were refugees from Saigon U. Now we are down to 2040; however, the "knob" percentage is the same.

The Citadel Hilton has acquired 2000 brand new beds with box springs and ten inch (honest) inner springs, have to have MC's and PP's now; also 1,000 new desks and 350 new chairs. It is hoped by September '67 to have everything new, except cadets.

General Harris likes to give amnesty, having given six in 11 months. The Corps and I really cooperate to keep him happy. One lamb earned 160 tours in 3 weeks and a friend of his 140 tours, so you can see we are trying.

As you may know Mrs. Clark died in October. There was a memorial service for her in Summerall Chapel well attended by cadets. We have lost 16 lambs in Viet Nam, Skip Murphy '65 being the latest. Cheer up, the good die young; you and I will be around a long time. But always remember, I'm going to be Sgt. of Lesesne Gate in Hell.

The same lamb, whom I took blue jeans off in the middle of the parade ground during Summer School, showed up at Christmas muster in civilian long tails and white tie. He had his coat and tie just like regulations state.

All the jock teams are playing hard even though they aren't winning all of them.

Colonel John Williams, Assistant Commandant, is retiring in June '67. He is a West Pointer who has been with The Citadel over 20 years and has helped the college in many ways.

My family, Miss Betsy and all The Citadel send our best regards to you and yours.

Boo

'67

Happy '67 Christmas Lambs,

The Ashley and the Cooper keep rolling along and so does El Cid. For the first time in 3 years, we started off in September only about 20 over in barracks. With all the new furniture in the rooms they are really crowded now. With 3 men rooms, you have to go outside to change your mind. With 4 men rooms, you can move around, and 2 men rooms are fat cats; more places to hide junk.

Major Freda, Dr. Cathcart, Colonel Warren Stutler and Colonel Causey all died during the past year. General Clark was married in October 1967. The new Chemistry Building is being built across from #4 Barracks and should be ready for use by September '68. Also the Alumni have a new house outside SOUTH Gate.

The Tactical Officers handle WEL's and C.P.'s in their Companies; it sure has been a help to me, no more late calls. Had our 8th suspension of punishment in September. However, the quad has not been empty. Cdr. Coussons is "Tac" to Company "Top" and is doing a good job. Can you picture "Tango" winning a parade? They did! Colonel John Williams retired last June and has been running all over the nation. This year General Harris let 5-year men live off the campus and be "Day Students." J. Bowditch, S. Dewey, Fletcher, etc.; what a blessing. The old green dragon is gone; I now operate a Blue '66 2-door low-priced Ford.

I know all of you will enjoy hearing that Dan Brailsford, '66, was caught non-brown-bagging at the Furman game; our future Governor.

My little girl is a soph at Medical College and Al is trying to catch up to be a Second Classman.

The Citadel has lost more than her fair share in Viet Nam this year, all fine, good, young men, so you lambs don't worry, you are too wicked to die. You will be back here wanting a pass or 3 merits.

The footballers played well, there just was not enough of them to go around for ten games. The new basketball Coach has them fired up. Can you picture Bridges or Cauthen excited? H. Read, Business Manager, is leaving 1 January '68.

We are still here trying to produce the "whole" man, but there is always something missing; a toe, finger, or a head.

My family, Miss Betsy, and I wish you a Merry Christmas and a Happy, Safe New Year.

Best always

Boo

'68

Dear Lambs:

We have had a few changes; General Tucker

was relieved in Feb. '68, Miss Betsy quit in Feb. '68 and I was relieved 1 May '68. Filled in for John Holliday as Provost Marshall until 1 Aug. John had quite a serious operation but has recovered real well and is doing fine. Dr. Sandifer & Miss Maloney have left the Hospital, Rembert J. '61 is in English, Moore J. R. '62 & Muller K. L. '66 are Asst. PMS's. I have heard that at least 9 Ph D's have joined the faculty.

I am now the Supply & Property Officer; it is "fat city" but I do miss the contact with cadets. I do have one big problem if I can clear up, it will be gone for good. I found 546 pieces of luggage belonging to cadets who have departed from The Citadel. I have sent out over 300 pieces but still have a hard core I can't find. Attached is a list, if you run into any of them. Please ask them to write for their luggage.

The football team was magnificent, good boys (no bums) playing hard, but we really were hurt in the legs and neck. At one time the top three linebackers could not play. Nine will require leg operations this year. Six made All-Southern and three made All State. Ken Diaz was on both of them and it was well deserved.

Basketball is getting off to a good start but we don't have any goons, our tallest duckbutt is 6'5". I don't know much of cadet life these days as I don't see them.

Tom Evans '68 (Co D) was killed in an auto wreck in Atlanta in Nov. '68, first of his class. We still have a lot in V.N. but Thank God not many killed or wounded. Goble '66 was wounded bad but has recovered and is still over there.

"Sandy" Kelly, widow of Bennie Kelly '61

KIA, V.N., presented The Citadel with a "Kelly Cup" for the best drilled squad awarded each year; in addition the Squad leader will get a medal.

Andy Latta, an animal if there ever was one, had his sister draw a charcoal portrait of me. It is one of the finest gifts I have ever received.

Incidentally, Latta, Coburn, Windham, all crack football players gave it up to study and all graduated with their class.

My office is in the luggage warehouse so I will be changing from a cariBoo to a Swamp Rat.

My wife is not too well, my little girl is doing well as a junior in Med school and Al needs 120 Q.P.'s; with the grace of God and a long-handle spoon he should make it in Aug. '69.

We all wish you the best.

                                        Boo

                                        '69

Dear Lamb:

1969 has been quite a year for me, besides the men walking on the moon. My son Al graduated in August so that's one worry I'll never have again. All my family except myself have been sick, but everyone is fine now except my wife.

The Corps is in good shape; '69 got an extra weeks' furlough last Christmas and had a girl in a parade, June week. '70 had a mob visit to Furman, they did too much damage and made the Furman football team mad but our cadets were quite shrewd.

Our football team was good, you won't see a better game anywheres the day we beat Davidson. The basketball team is young but is hustling. We play our first basketball game with Vanderbilt this year and our first football game in Sep. '70 with Vanderbilt.

The new Chemistry Building SW of Bond Hall is a dream, even you could pass chemistry in Byrd Hall. The West wing of Bond Hall is completely down and is being rebuilt. For the past two years and the next two, 4th Bn won't be able to hear an artillery barrage come in, when they leave The Cid.

We lost some mighty good boys this past year.

'68 T. H. Evans, C. A. Peterson
'67 F. J. Carter MIA, G. L. Miner, N. A. Rowe, Jr., B. R. Welge
'63 E. M. Collins, Jr.

The good part is that some of our biggest bums, and I do mean bums, have gone out and have done well. I wouldn't have enlisted them in the Salvation Army.

We have a lot more beds than bodies this year, so if you can send something warm down here please do, not quite as shiftless as you were but some body to fill a bed and pay the tuition.

The Citadel will be on College Bowl (TV) Mar. 8, 1970; hold both of them for us.

Saw Miss Betsy about two weeks ago and she is fine.

I have the best job I ever had in my life but I miss the Lambs.

With all the best wishes for a New Year.

Boo

Afterthoughts

The next letter was sent to Cadet Dave Savarene in 1964. Cadet Savarene came to The Boo as soon as he got the letter, swore he had not been frequenting Charleston brothels, and could not understand how the underworld had put him on its mailing list. The Boo racked him about loose morals and sins of the flesh, then told him he was the victim of a cadet prank. Greatly relieved, Savarene left the letter with Boo and departed from his office determined to lead the righteous life.

The letter goes:

> 198 Market Street
> Charleston, S.C.
> January 11, 1964

Cadet Dave Savarene
Citadel Military College
Charleston, South Carolina

Dear Cadet Savarene:

We were extremely pleased to hear of your interest in our new business. It is located, as you probably know, at 198 Market Street. We understand that it may be your wish to do business with us. Before you commit yourself any further, we wish you to understand more about our establishment.

Our establishment is not of ordinary caliber. You will find that it is clean above ordinary standards of cleanliness. Our girls believe in cleanliness before godliness. Our employees have the desire to please all mankind.

We feel that our girls are not here just to make a living . . . they are, in a sense, here to be a boost to all mankind. If a man is not satisfied in his sexual life, it makes sense that he will be high-strung, nervous, and in general, hard to get along with. It is our business to fulfill that need.

A cadet often needs relations with girls because of their continuous male environment. The weekend is his release for these pent up emotions . . . and these emotions must be spent. If you are going with a girl, you do not want the possibility of having an illegitimate child. You have your education to think of and you would not want to endanger it, we are sure. Because of this, you should come to our establishment. Your safety from disease is insured because of the high standards of cleanliness we proclaim.

Our girls are clean, wholesome, and well-versed in the skill of love-making. They are not unexperienced!! They are well trained and it is to your advantage to come to us.

The price is well within your range. Ask your friends to come with you for a very enjoyable evening worth every penny you pay!!

There is no need to worry about having to make love to pigs because we pride ourselves in having some of the most gorgeous girls in the south. Their figures are truly God's own creation!

Sincerely yours,

/s/ J. P. McDonald

J. P. McDonald

Director of Social Events

*

The next letter is from Anita Murphy. She wrote The Boo after her son received a punishment order. The Boo loved the spirit of the woman and wished out loud that every Citadel parent shared her attitude.

Dublin, Georgia
December 17, 1962

Lt. Colonel T. N. Courvoisie
The Citadel
Charleston, South Carolina

Dear Sir:

Regarding your letter of December 12, 1962, if The Citadel Censor, in this particular case, happens to be one Cadet David Murphy, then you have my full permission to turn him over on the other side and paddle the daylights out of him. I have very little respect for an informer and if I were physically able, I would take care of him personally. You have my deepest sympathy, sir, for having to be subjected to the endless antics of boys like my son and parents like me.

I am very happy to learn that David is in excellent health. That would seem to indicate that his ulcer has healed over. Also, since he has loads of time to study and there are no young (or old) women to disturb him, then he won't be needing my car and you can tell him to send it home, because I get awfully cold walking to work every day.

We wish for you and yours a very Merry Christmas and hope that you won't be too

lonely or that things won't be too dull while
"Little Dave" and the other boys are away.

Apologetically yours,
/s/ Anita B. Murphy
Anita B. Murphy

★

The cadets who walked tours formed a kind
of fraternity of their own. The fifty-minute
walk, back and forth across the second battalion quadrangle, cemented many friendships
that ordinarily would never have been made.
This was a fraternity of lawbreakers and
inveterate challengers of the system. They
walked tours together, they laughed together,
they joked with The Boo together, and after
their punishment was served, they drank beer
together. The Boo knew these cadets as well as
he knew any on campus. They exchanged
wisecracks. They bantered each other
mercilessly. The miscreants who walked tours
were proud of their relationship with The Boo.
Tom McDow was prouder than most. In order
to preserve the traditions of the perennial tour-
walkers, McDow drew up the following
document:

THE SOUTH CAROLINA CORPS OF CADETS
The Citadel, Charleston, S.C.

29 September 1962

SUBJECT: Request for authority to form a
           cadet drill team known as "The
           Caribou Raiders."
THROUGH: The Commandant of Cadets
TO: The President

1. I request authority to hold a meeting on Saturday 29 September 1962 on the quadrangle on Number Two Barracks of all tour-walking cadets who are interested in forming a cadet drill team to be called the Caribou Raiders.

2. The purpose of this drill team shall be:
   a. to honor the good shepherd, Lt. Colonel T. N. Courvoisie, who has done an outstanding job of handling his lambs.
   b. to add color to all tour formations so that they will reflect greater credit on The Citadel and the great association of privates.
   c. to improve the drill of senior privates.
   d. to provide entertainment for visitors on Homecoming Day, Parents' Day, Corps Day, and the birthday of Lt. Colonel Courvoisie.
   e. to plan social activities that will tighten the bonds of friendship formed on the quad and also to insure that members do not long remain off the squad.

3. At this organization meeting, it is proposed that officers will be elected as the group desires and that a constitution will be approved by the membership. The action taken at this meeting will be reported to the authorities of The Citadel through channels for final approval.

4. I am familiar with General Order 20, Headquarters of The Citadel, dated 19 February 1962 and *Blue Book Regulations 13.01; 12.02; 13.03;* and 13.04. If this request is granted, no advantage will be taken of these or other *Blue Book* Regulations.

★

Once in a while the cadet would raise his voice in a song of agony. He would do it for no other reason than to be heard. He needed pity for a single moment. Whether he was serving confinements or walking tours, the lamentation which issued from his mouth was an indication that the pressure was getting too much. Cadet Black wrote his poem in a bleak frame of mind and sent it to The Boo. The Boo's reply is written below. Two poets locked in combat. What is lacking in meter is made up for in emotion. The Boo-poem proves that the Colonel was wise in choosing the Army as a career instead of literature. But the cadets loved these word battles. Even if his verse was suspect, The Boo never lost one of these matches.

Confinements

Many an hour at my desk I sit
Wishing like hell I hadn't pulled that shit
Cursing the system and raising hell
And swearing in the future I shall do well
For all wrongs committed one has to pay
In cadet tradition, what can I say
But from it all a lesson is taught
If you do something wrong dammit
don't get caught!!!
"67"
BLACK

(handwritten)

You are so right
And you would look bright
at Joe College where you would
Always be right.
/s/ Boo

The Green Comet

An ugly car. No doubt about it, a very ugly car. It was squat and awkward, a car neither to be raced or exhibited with pride, but a car which became the most immediately recognizable symbol of discipline on The Citadel's campus. The General's car displayed several waving flags. It was brash and imposing—a black Cadillac that reminded one of wreaths and funerals. The cadets ignored the General's car, for it was commonly conceded among the Corps that you could be raping a Vestal Virgin and never merit a glance from the exalted eyes in the back of the great Cadillac. The green Comet called for vigilance. Usually when you saw it, it was already past you or coming up to you. Its pace was slow and determined as it wound through the well planned environs of The Citadel, as it circumnavigated the parade ground, or cut behind the barracks to intercept cadets intent on a stolen day in Charleston. The cadet knew this car like he knew the face of his mother, the bark of his dog, or the sound of reveille at 6:15 in the morning.

It had character. If given rank, most assuredly the title of senior private would be bestowed upon it. A sloppy, disheveled car in a world of Impalas and Super Sports. A relaxed car, strolling the campus unhurriedly, seeing what could be seen in the tiny universe to which it was confined; a car where justice sat, where judge and jury smoked a long, long cigar and awarded punishments for scuffed shoes and corroded brass. The Boo's car could drive by a whole company of cadets and elicit cries of "Hey Boo" from a hundred sources. A car which sometimes swung out of Lesesne Gate and followed the railroad tracks to The Ark, where scores of cadets have met a Waterloo. A place where many cadets have exited with bellies afire to find themselves facing the inscrutable headlights of the Green Comet and the faint glow of a Tampa Nugget illuminating the steering wheel.

The Green Comet became a landmark, a touchstone universally accepted by cadets as a symbol of The Citadel. Cadets at home on Christmas or Easter Furlough would see a similar car pass them in Cordele, Georgia, or Pen Yann, New York, and the reaction would be the same. Their heads would turn instinctively to see if by some chance, some blind miracle that it was The Boo's car they saw. When they returned to the campus, they would stop Colonel Courvoisie to tell him they thought about him during furlough.

The Citadel Museum could never collect any item which could define and embody a group of years so well as the car The Boo drove. The car became a symbol of the man and ultimately of the school. The car itself represented the discipline which separated The Citadel from other schools. It also caught the spirit of the school itself: a trifle eccentric, a little odd, yet possessing a character and fascination all of its own. The cadets would wave at the car and the man inside would wave back. That's the way it should be. That's the way it always was.

Of and About Musuems

The Citadel Musuem is a sterile, quiet place where nice, dedicated people gather to preserve history behind glass cases and locked doors. Cadets usually go there once in their career at The Citadel and never go again. The museum is financed so poorly and supported so inadequately by the school itself that it is a tribute to the dedication of the staff that the museum has survived at all.

One problem the museum has always had in the eyes of some cadets is its worship of General Mark Clark. One whole room of the museum is dedicated to the propagation of Clark's exploits through two wars. The room itself is dark, an inner sanctum lit with tabernacle lights, and smoking with a kind of mystical incense which seems to complement the godly aura of the man himself. One display case shows the pair of pants Clark wore on a spy mission to North Africa. In the next case the visitor fully expects to see the jock strap Clark wore during an intra-mural volleyball game at West Point. Statues of Clark, pictures of Clark, letters from Clark, letters to Clark, speeches by Clark, and a seemingly endless amount of Clark memorabilia helps make the museum a monument to his career. If any pictures were available of Clark walking on water or changing wine into water, they would dutifully be placed in the museum by people who suffer guilt feelings that The Citadel has never produced an international figure of its own. Instead of the musuem being a reflection of the cadets and of cadet life, it has become a reflection of The Citadel as some would like to have her projected to the world: a signer of peace treaties, a victor in major battles, an important force in the affairs of the world. The unique flavor of cadet life has been preserved only in a couple of displays and they constitute the most significant portion of the museum itself.

When visitors come to The Citadel Musuem for a look into the life of The Citadel or a leisurely peek into cadet traditions, they miss the finest collection of cadet history, lore, and memorabilia on campus. If they wanted to know about cadets at their creative, don't give a damn, let's get-the-system best, they would come to The Boo's office.

Boo's office is cluttered with cadet contra-band covering a ten-year period. Cartoons, ERW's, nametags, newspapers, books and a hundred other assorted items line the wall and give his office the appearance of a broken-down pawn shop. Here he keeps the things for which he remembers cadets the most: their rebellion against the system, their efforts to find identity in The Citadel world of gray, their unflagging spirit, and their ability to find humor in any and every situation that arose. The list I give is incomplete, but fairly representative.

One cadet, fairly weary of The Citadel's restrictions, presented The Boo with a statue of Mickey Mouse dressed splendidly in a Citadel Shako and Pom-pom.

★

Cadet Powell from Florence gave Boo the head of a stuffed snarling bobcat another cadet had stolen from a beer joint on the Savannah Highway.

★

A fake package, owned by Malvin Glass, addressed to his father, Colonel Glass, sat on his bookshelf for four years. The package was neatly wrapped in brown paper and tied with string, and stamped with the proper amount of postage. The bottom was false, however, and this innocent, but official-looking box sheltered Cadet Glass's coffee pot for four long years. Drinking coffee gave human pleasure and was forbidden cadets in the barracks.

★

A rubber stamp saying "Drop Dead" which The Boo occasionally used on ERW's when he thought the cadet was trying to dazzle him with unnecessary footwork.

★

Colonel Courvoisie's own Shako which he saved from his cadet days at The Citadel.

★

A favorite phrase of The Boo's when administering justice to some offending or offensive cadet was to "bust your gonads, Bubba." One cadet gave The Boo a wooden mallet and a rounded ball to aid in such an undertaking.

★

One cadet presented Boo with a can of Professor Willoughby's World Famous Bullcrap Repellent to help prevent and cure cases of Bullcrapping. The directions on the can read, "When Bullcrap is detected, aim atomizer at source and spray for one second." Professor Willoughby suggests his patented B.S. shovel for chronic cases.

★

Cadet Vriezlaar presented The Boo his removable car sticker which could be taken off his car as soon as he left campus.

★

A silver cup presented to The Boo by the Class of 1961 making him an honorary member.

★

Mock newspaper headlines from cadets debauching at the Mardi Gras in New Orleans. "Cadets Molest Virgins on Bourbon Street," reads one. Another announces, "Colonel Courvoisie Arrives In Town: Red Light District Reopens."

★

A statue of Napoleon sits high above The Boo's desk. This is the emblem of Courvoisier brandy and a thoroughly inebriated member of the Summerall Guards heisted it from a bar in New Orleans, scratched out the "R" and brought it home for The Boo.

★

The largest item ever to sit in The Boo's makeshift museum was a twelve-foot aluminum boat which a cadet had brought illegally into the barracks.

★

On the wall hangs a portrait of The Boo drawn by George O'Kelly of the Class of 1965. Beside it sits a certificate naming The Boo "Tac Officer Emeritus of The Regimental Band."

★

Jimbo Plunkett, shipped by The Boo for excessive demerits, sent The Boo a flag on March 17 declaring him an official Irishman.

★

A huge bronzed shoe worn by Thomas McDow through 120 tours and presented to The Boo as a gift when the tours were completed.

★

A basketball player, with a jaundiced view of The Citadel and her traditions, painted his shako a bright silver and kept it on display in his room for two years—until The Boo inspected his room one night.

★

A neatly bound book entitled "How to Fool The Boo by Colonel Courvoisie." A cadet's father owned a printing shop and had the book sent to Colonel Courvoisie as a gift. One opens the book and finds 250 blank pages to study.

★

One whole shelf of The Boo's bookcase is covered by false nametags worn by cadets at The Citadel over a period of years. Since every cadet had to wear a nametag at all times when he was wandering around the campus, it was inevitable that some cadets would wear names which reflected their own particular philosophy or attitude toward The Citadel or themselves. The most popular false nametag The Boo encountered was the one which proudly said, "Mr. Military." Some of the others have been: Agammemnon, Budweiser, Wildman, Bones, Moon, Yogi, Inefficient, Polar Bear, Clod, Study, Fat Elf, and Degenerate.

A cadet presented The Boo with a navel salt cellar. When The Boo protested that he had no stinking idea what to do with a goddamn navel salt cellar the cadet patiently explained, "Colonel, you stick this little, tiny cup into your bellybutton. You then pour a little salt into the little cup. Then you get a couple of sticks of celery, dip it in the salt, and watch T.V."

"Thanks a million, Bubba," said Boo.

A kitchen match box, when opened, reveals an exact replica of a Citadel bed fully made and ready for inspection. Inside the match box is the inscription, "A portable Beauty Rest to take a nap between classes in pursuit of the Rip Van Winkle Habit."

★

Intricately carved waist plates by Bill Leffler describing the punishment orders he served:

"Firearms in Barracks, 3 Dec. 1966, W. A. Leffler."

Every time Bill received a punishment order The Boo received a waist plate.

★

The mother of Dave Murphy was absolutely, unabashedly delighted when the system caught up with her son and The Boo gave him a punishment order. She sent Colonel Courvoisie a whole box of materials to give her son: paper money "for paying off the Commandant and buying back your stripes," 44 dot-to-dot pictures to help while away the time during Saturday night confinements, and Dr. Scholl's footpads to prevent sore feet from walking tours.

★

A huge, graphically illustrated invitation "To Da Boo" drawn by Johnny Law, inviting the Colonel to the graduation exercises of all senior bums. Inside, a senior private with a torn, filthy uniform and flies swarming around his head stood in mock attention.

★

A replica of a cannon which also served to light The Boo's cigar.

★

Three scrapbooks filled with ERW's written by cadets whose minds remained fresh and creative within the system.

★

A trowel and a picture of a doorway completely bricked up to remind the casual visitor of Bob Wenhold's and Larry Kurtz's famous attempt to seal up their first sergeant in his room. The first sergeant, overcome by his own importance, was making it tough on the underclassmen in his company. Early one Sunday morning, Bob and Larry crept down the gallery with an enormous load of material and proceeded to brick up every inch of their first sergeant's door. They hoped the authorities at The Citadel could not break down their wall until the first sergeant had time enough to starve to death. Unfortunately, when the surprised first sergeant opened his door the next morning, he was able to burst his way out of his room. The cement had not had time enough to harden.

★

Peter Them provided a recent addition to The Boo's collection. Upon returning from Viet Nam, Pete came to Colonel Courvoisie's house. The Colonel wasn't there so Pete presented his gift to Mrs. Courvoisie. It was a rifle taken from a dead Viet Cong infantry man. On the rifle was a gold plaque with the inscription, "To The Boo with fondest regards. Peter Them '67."

After he gave it to Mrs. Courvoisie, Pete cleared his throat and said, "Mrs. Courvoisie, don't misunderstand me. I want the Colonel to live for a long time, but when he dies, can I have the rifle back?"

More Bits and Pieces

Tim Belk was the first recorded cadet ever to bleach his hair while at The Citadel. He was also the first cadet ever to receive a punishment for it.

★

A nervous cadet named Roderman had a punishment order rescinded. He brought the Assistant Commandant a note from a doctor saying he would probably die if he walked any more tours. His stomach ulcers were so bad the doctor feared for Cadet Roderman's life if he continued to pace back and forth across the second battalion quadrangle. After much deliberation, the Commandant's Department rescinded the order.

★

Sam Dufford wished to put the military skills he developed at The Citadel to immediate use. Since the United States, unfortunately, was fighting no war at the time of Dufford's graduation, he went to the hills of Cuba and became one of Fidel Castro's most trusted advisors. He later wrote a book on his experiences there.

★

Spit-shined, heel-clicking, ultra sharp, gung-ho Joel Moore was practicing sword manual before his mirror one night. While returning his sword to the sheath one time, Joel missed completely and made a two-foot slit down his leg instead. Poor Joel found it difficult living amidst the snickering congregation of privates and five-year men forevermore.

★

Some of the Band Company boys discovered that the street between Number 1 and Number 2 barracks had no name. In the dark of the night they grunted and panted their way out of the North Sallyport of Padgett-Thomas Barracks carrying an extremely heavy and official looking street marker. When they finally crept back to their rooms, they had succeeded in naming a street without official sanction. When the band gathers in white and gray, with gleaming horn and polished drum, in full splendor to begin the Friday parade, the first roll of the drum begins on "Courvoisie Boulevard" and "Via Freda."

★

Every year on his birthday, General Clark granted amnesty to the cadets. This habit soon became tradition and the cadets with punishment orders or confinements eagerly awaited the first day of May each year. Toward the end of Clark's tenure as president, five cadets decided to take advantage of Clark's benevolent disposition on the celebration of his birthday. Two weeks before the feast day five shadows left the campus illegally and did not return for four days. They drank enough beer and chased enough women to satisfy their desire for the more salient pleasures of civilian life. They returned to campus giggling and confident that they would walk tours for one weekend and then be a part of Clark's general amnesty the following week. When The Boo figured out the game, however, he sat on the order for two weeks, taking no action whatsoever. The five walked no tours the following weekend. Their punishment finally came out on May 2, a brief twenty-four hours after Clark granted amnesty to the grateful Corps. C. B. Taylor's father wrote The Boo an iceberg of a letter asking why he had not acted upon the offense as soon as it was reported. And though the boys complained bitterly and claimed unfair treatment, they became familiar figures at tour formation in second battalion.

★

Boo's biggest weekend for bailing out cadet lawbreakers came in the spring of 1967. On Friday night the police called The Boo at his home. They said a Cadet Dustin was cooling off in the Charleston jail and The Boo could come get him for a mere 300 dollars. Dustin, a big-biceped jock, had resisted arrest, assaulted a policeman and disturbed the peace. Boo went and bailed him out. The next night two more cadets insulted a couple of policemen and The Boo made the familiar trek to the station to retrieve them. Bail was set at 100 dollars for each of them. On Sunday morning of the same weekend, Terry Dervan's girl friend called The Boo and begged him to bail Terry out of jail. Boo calmed the girl down, got into the green Comet and went to Dervan's aid. He had sassed a policeman who picked him up for speeding. Properly chastened, Boo brought him back to the campus. Sunday afternoon, the desk sergeant called Boo for the fifth time that weekend.

"Colonel, this is Sergeant Adamson again. Yep, we got another one. This kid was speeding, driving without a license, and sassing a police officer. Can you come get him?" "Yes, Sir. I'll be right down."

When the weekend was over, Boo had freed five cadets on sight recognition. Total bail was over 600 dollars.

The Boo says he was 44 years old before he knew a Chief of Police and then he became acquainted with five of them. In taking care of cadets and summer school students The Boo found it difficult at times to raise 300 dollars on a Sunday morning to bail a few "lambs" out of jail. He established contact with all Chiefs of Police in the area and with their cooperation worked out the following solution. The Boo would be notified as soon as a cadet was apprehended for speeding, fighting, etc. The Boo could have a cadet released on sight recognition, return him to barracks and then produce the culprit in time for court.

In addition to protecting the cadets, where possible, against court charges on their records (the services are wary of awarding commissions to people with court records) the authorities were generally agreeable to dropping a 25 dollar fine in exchange for 10/60/3 months restriction awarded by The Citadel.

★

Five-year men did not give a crap about the
military traditions and responsibilites inherent
in a Citadel education. After all, it was only a
miscarriage of justice they were still at the
school; and their classmates had already begun
their careers, married their sweethearts, and
commenced to live like ordinary human beings.
So a certain amount of residual bitterness
rested in the soul of each five-year man on
campus. When The Boo took over as Assistant
Commandant he immediately saw the five-year
man would be most likely to skip parade, sleep
through chapel, or sneak out to Charleston for a
quick beer. To alleviate the alienation of fifth-
year men somewhat, The Boo instituted a policy
which enjoyed immediate and gratifying
success. He took the salute gun detail, the
group of cadets responsible for firing the
cannon at parade, and filled its ranks completely with five-year men. This, in fact,
became the only criterion for membership in
the group—that your shadow had graced The
Citadel campus past the date when the rest of
your class left the campus. The psychological
impact on these men was considerable. A five-
year man whose appearance reminded one of a
perfect blend between a custodian and a grave
digger suddenly blossomed into a shining
picture-postcard image of the perfect cadet.
Others who had skipped as many parades as
there were Fridays became prompt and eager at
the parade formations. They cut their hair,
shined their shoes, and performed their task
efficiently and with conspicuous pride. All of
which supported one of The Boo's dusty
theories: that every man, no matter how

disreputable or undesirable he seems, needs to belong and to function and to contribute something valuable to the effort of the entire group.

★

Young girl crying on the phone. Great heaving sobs.

"I'm pregnant. That son of a bitch, Cadet Varlenti, won't marry me. I thought a cadet was a gentleman. He promised me, Colonel, he promised me."

This is a facsimile of a conversation The Boo received sometime in 1961. If a cadet became a surprised father and left the surprised and expectant mother to cast her fate to the many prevailing winds of Charleston, The Boo would often receive hysterical phone calls demanding justice from the reluctant cadet. In this case, as in all the others, The Boo called five cadets into Jenkins Hall. The cadets remained downstairs at strict attention. He brought the girl out of his office (she had dressed to the teeth for this event). Together they stood upstairs looking at the five cadets. Boo had selected four of them at random from the Corps. One of them was Cadet Varlenti.

"Right face," The Boo roared.

"Left face," he roared again.

"Which one is it, honey?" The Boo asked.

"I don't know, Colonel."

She could not pick out the cadet who supposedly had fathered her child.

★

A mother called Colonel Courvoisie one afternoon just before Corps Day. She said, "Colonel, I hate to bother you but I just had to call someone. My daughter is seventeen and has been dating Cadet J for about a month. He is the first boy she has ever dated. Well, Colonel, he invited her to the Corps Day Hop with him. I can't begin to tell you how thrilled she was. We went downtown to buy a dress. We found one that was absolutely beautiful. It was expensive, but we both loved it. Then she had her hair fixed for the prom. And all of her girl friends know about it. Well, Colonel, Cadet J called last night and broke the date. My daughter didn't go to school today because . . . well . . . I had to call somebody."

"Madame," The Boo answered. "I may be able to help you."

At the Corps Day Hop, Colonel and Mrs. Courvoisie stood in the receiving line. When Cadet J and his date passed by, Mrs. Courvoisie couldn't help but remark to her husband that the girl was wearing a particularly attractive dress.

★

Harry Lester was a bum from the very first day he entered Lesesne Gate to the very last. He was a discipline problem in the highest, purest sense of the term. He and The Boo squared off several times during his infamous years as a cadet. But one of The Boo's greatest surprises as Assistant Commandant came several years after Harry graduated, when Harry called and said, "Colonel, I think it is a disgrace to The Citadel for cadets to be going around Charleston with 'El Cid' stickers on their windows. Can you do something about it? If they aren't proud enough to put Citadel stickers on their cars, then keep them in on the weekends."

From that moment on The Boo believed in the resurrection and regeneration of bums.

★

George Garbade looked like the typical jock, sort of square-shaped, thick-trunked and powerful. He played fullback on the football team and achieved a certain amount of success. Like many jocks, his feet were faster than his brain, and he found himself in summer school after the rest of his class had graduated in June. Toward the middle of August, George started acting a little funny. He would lie in bed for days at a time, staring at the ceiling in absolute silence, or babbling incoherently to no one in particular. His roommate, becoming extremely concerned, went to The Boo's house one night to ask for advice. The Boo went over to see George himself. When The Boo came into the room, Garbade never looked up, just lay on his back, with a glazed and sightless expression, not saying anything to anybody. When The Boo spoke to him, no response whatsoever registered in George's eyes and he gave no indication that anything The Boo said to him got past the wall he had erected between himself and the world. George snapped out of it in time to take and pass his exams. He and his roommate came over to the Courvoisie house to say goodbye. While saying appropriate farewells, George slipped his Citadel ring from his finger. "Colonel, take this ring. I don't deserve to wear it."

The Boo took the ring. George's roommate came back later and said he would get George to take it back.

The Boo never learned what was eating George, what restless, ineluctable guilt lived inside of him that he could not verbalize or release. He wanted to talk, he wanted to expurgate his guilt, and he wanted to do some symbolic act in retribution, this The Boo was sure of. He never found out. For George never came back.

★

Poor, skinny Ulysses S. Simmons distinguished himself the very first week he was at The Citadel. Now anyone whose first name and subsequent initial summon up visions of the general who humbled Robert E. Lee is going to find it hard plowing in the school which prides itself on firing the first shot of the Civil War. Ulysses indeed felt the grinning corporals with the grits and gravy voices were tougher on him than on the other freshmen. The whole system upset him so much, in fact, that on the fourth morning he was at The Citadel he woke up feeling strangely, looked in the mirror, and saw that he was bracing for no reason. When he tried to relax, he found that he could not, that he had lost all control of his throat muscles and that no matter how hard he tried, his chin remained rigidly tucked against his throat. This worried Ulysses a great deal. When the upperclassmen learned of his malady, they hooted and hollered, giggled and snickered at poor Ulysses twice as vigorously as they had before.

They ordered him to relax, to stand "at ease," to stick his chin out as far as he could—all to no avail, for the chin of Ulysses remained fixed and riveted in the bracing position. After great deliberation, Ulysses went to the hospital for treatment. Doctor Hugh Cathcart scratched his head, admitted puzzlement, muttered something about psychology and mental chaos, and put Ulysses to bed. Ulysses braced in his sleep and when he was awake, when he ate breakfast and when he went to the bathroom. He was not goldbricking. Finally, through an act of God, the involuntary bracing stopped after seven days. Ulysses went back to the Corps with considerable fame and notoriety earned from his strange and unexplained week. All the generals, the colonels, the secretaries, and the street cleaners on campus knew the story of Ulysses, the knob who couldn't stop bracing.

The Boo had met Ulysses on one of his daily visits to the hospital and asked him how he was getting along. They had chatted every day that week. When it was over, The Boo had made a friend for a four-year period. The only requirement Boo had passed in the eyes of Ulysses was kindness and concern when the world about him mocked the name and eccentricity of Ulysses S. Simmons.

So they became friends. After a disconcerting beginning Ulysses started to adjust to the life in the corps. He talked to Colonel Courvoisie every time they met on campus and even went over to see The Boo and his wife at night, just to chat and swap stories, if nothing else. The boy wanted someone to talk to, this was obvious to both Colonel and Mrs. Courvoisie, so they encouraged his visits. After a year or two of visiting and becoming comfortable in the Courvoisie household, Ulysses related how the tension between him and his father was becoming almost unbearable, that the father barely spoke to him at home, and that the father was very displeased that Ulysses was very unathletic and had failed to gain rank in the Corps of Cadets. True, Simmons did not gain immense popularity at The Citadel. A tinge of effeminacy did little to bolster his status among cadets very conscious of the masculine image they felt a military school should project. He never got rank. Nor did he ever make an athletic squad. But he did several things at The Citadel which The Boo felt Mr. Simmons should recognize.

Ulysses won gold stars at The Citadel for two consecutive semesters, no small feat in a school where the spit-shined shoe is often more admired than the quality point. He also was an avid participant in the intramural program in his company, and even though he was basically one of the poorest athletes ever produced above the Mason-Dixon line, he tried like hell to play whatever sport was in season. But Mr. Simmons was not interested in any accomplishments of his older son. He was more concerned with Ulysses' younger brother, an athletic, handsome kid four years younger than Ulysses. The younger boy was a star halfback on his high school football team and very popular with everyone at the school. The younger son represented and embodied everything Mr. Simmons had hoped for in Ulysses; the younger son, in essence, was the son Mr. Simmons had wanted and finally gotten. He simply didn't give a damn about Ulysses.

In November of his senior year, Ulysses came over to the Courvoisie house looking a bit more dejected than usual.

"What's wrong, Bubba? You look like judgment day is here and gone."

"Colonel, it's the Ring Hop," Simmons answered.

"Don't you have a date? We can arrange that if you want."

"No, Colonel, I have a date. Mom's coming down to watch me go through the ring. My grandfather is coming, too. But Dad isn't coming, Colonel."

"Why not, Bubba? Is he sick, dead, or just dying?"

"None of those. My brother has a football game that night and Dad doesn't want to miss it."

"Well, that's a shame, Bubba, I'm awful sorry."

"I just wanted to tell you, Colonel."

"Thanks, Ulysses."

The next day Colonel Courvoisie called Mrs. Simmons on the phone. He called hesitatingly. He had a habit of calling parents who were putting too much pressure on their sons and asking them to lay off a bit. At any time the parent could tell him to go to hell or go flush himself down the nearest commode and there would be nothing he could do about it. But he usually called anyway.

Mrs. Simmons answered the phone.

"Hello, Madame. This is Courvoisie of The Citadel."

"Is Ulysses in trouble?" Mrs. Simmons asked in a frantic, customary maternal response.

"I don't think so, Mrs. Simmons. But he might be. He came over to my house last night a little upset. He said his father wasn't coming to the Ring Hop because he wanted to see his other son play a football game."

"Yes, Colonel, I tried to talk to my husband, but he doesn't seem to understand."

"Yes, Ma'am, I understand. Maybe you should try to tell him how important the Ring Hop is to the cadet, what it means to him and what is should mean to a cadet's parents. Your son has been greatly hurt by your husband, Madame. I just called to see if you could persuade your husband to give up one football game for the sake of his oldest son. I think it would do Ulysses a great deal of good. He loves his father very much, but doesn't seem to think his father feels the same way."

"I'll try to persuade him, Colonel. Thanks so much for calling."

The next night Ulysses walked through the ring with his girl. His mother was very proud. So was his father, even though he later went back to his motel room to call his younger son to see who won the game.

A corollary to the story of Ulysses: Ulysses won a scholarship to graduate school after he graduated from The Citadel. The younger brother came to The Citadel as a freshman a year later. He played mediocre football and performed disastrously in the classroom. He flunked out in his sophomore year.

★

Cadet Graubart was one of the most creative salesmen ever to peddle sandwiches at The

Citadel. He perfected what he considered a fool proof method for making money selling sandwiches without getting busted by the Commandant's Department. He would take all his sandwiches and put them on the bench in the shower room. He placed a cigar box beside the sandwiches. Famished cadets could walk in the shower room, put their money in the cigar box, and take one sandwich. Meanwhile, Graubert had removed his pants and was sitting on a commode doing his homework and watching his profits soar. He sat on the commode for three hours each night. The only occupational hazard he noticed was a tendency for his behind to go to sleep.

Kroghie Andressen, nationally ranked punter for the football team, was the official pigeon-killer of Padgett-Thomas Barrack in the off season. Kroghie was such a disaster militarily, but such a deadly marksman, that The Boo figured he could be of some service to The Citadel by thinning out the pigeons who left their feces in so many conspicuous places around the campus.

One night Colonel and Mrs. Courvoisie were returning to campus when they spotted a cadet's car parked just outside the gates. Whenever cadets got itchy feet or the restless urge to depart after Taps and All-In, they would station their cars outside the campus perimeter, then follow the railroad tracks to the relative safety of Hampton Park. From there, the wine and lusts of Charleston were easily available. The Boo knew this ploy well. The sticker on the car showed this particular cadet was a Company Commander with the improbable name of Casey Batt. At nine o'clock, Cadet Batt received a phone call.

"Bubba, is your car parked off campus?"

"Yes, Sir."

"Bubba, were you planning to sneak off campus after lights were out tonight?"

"Yes, Sir."

"Well, Bubba, I wouldn't do that if I were you."

"No, Sir. I won't, Sir."

When Cadet Batt hung up his roommate asked who was calling.

"That was The Boo telling me not to sneak off campus tonight."

"How in the hell did he know?"

"I don't know, but he sure doesn't want me to go."

The roommate never believed him.

★

Cadet Ron Ellison, having devised the perfect plan for getting out of confinements, stormed confidently into the Colonel's office one Thursday afternoon. Ellison, an acknowledged wit, was in one of his initial forays into the world of The Boo and had heard by rumor that The Boo admired brashness and creative approaches by cadets inspired by the necessity of getting away from The Citadel on weekends. Therefore, he had practiced his line well.

"Colonel," he said, "you've got to postpone my confinements this weekend. I'll do anything.

I'll wash your car, mow your lawn, or date your ugly daughter.''

With this, The Boo leapt from his seat and nose to nose said to Ron, ''What ugly daughter are you talking about? My daughter is as pretty as any girl you've ever seen.''

Meekly, very meekly, the young lamb whispered, ''Colonel, I didn't know you had a daughter.'' With this, he slinked out of the room.

A green nightgown, which The Boo still wears, was forthcoming. A kind of peace offering from one who had survived.

Cadet Benny Kern rushed into The Boo's office waving a telegram which said that Mrs. Kern was sick in the hospital. The Boo said he knew for sure that Benny's mother was not in the hospital and refused to let him go on emergency leave. Benny introduced his wife to the Colonel on graduation day.

Courvoisie's sense of the dramatic sometimes got the best of him. To break the doldrums of winter tour formations, The Boo had two bandsmen exchange rifles for drums. They beat a steady, evocative cadence for two solid hours enlivening a dull and tedious exercise of cadet discipline.

Courvoisie was walking across the parade ground one afternoon when he spotted a figure two hundred feet away from him. The figure wore a grey hat, so The Boo instantly thought a cadet was out of uniform. He yelled the good yell, froze the cadet in mid-step, bawled him out, then apologized when he realized the boy was a visiting keydet from VMI, reputedly a military school between Charleston and West Point.

★

Band Company had two traditions which were honored by her members religiously. One was an annual occurrence. The Band Company knobs would wake up at 3 A.M., blow the bugle for reveille, then race back for their rooms as bleary-eyed upperclassmen stumbled out of their rooms to begin a new day. The sweat parties after the celebration of this tradition were also legendary.

The other tradition was a bit more specialized. Every fourth year, the seniors would initiate a crackdown on the under three classes. They would go through the rooms of the juniors, tear them apart, throw laundry on the floor, rip open presses, tear the beds to pieces, and give each junior fifteen or twenty demerits so their visit would be remembered. The sophomores and freshmen fared as poorly. The seniors then inspected the furious underclassmen at formation, burned them for improperly shined shoes, smudged brass, and wrinkled trousers. For two weeks this harassment continued. The juniors and sophomores rankled under this pressure. They cursed and mumbled expletives under their breaths. They planned mutinies, uprisings and murders. At the end of

two weeks, the seniors invited the entire
company to the company commander's room.
The company commander then informed the
underclassmen that the prior two weeks had
been a joke, the demerits did not count and the
seniors were treating the entire company to a
party. The seniors then brought in several cakes
and cases of soft drinks to appease the anger
and smooth the feathers of their subordinates.

★

J. C. Hare is a lawyer in Charleston who
graduated from The Citadel. Whenever a cadet
ran afoul of the law, The Boo sent the cadet to
Mr. Hare. Hare helped twenty or thirty cadets
out of jams and charged them nothing for his
services.

★

The Tourist Club was one of Boo's most
popular creations during his reign as Assistant
Commandant. A cadet won membership in the
Tourist Club after he had walked 100 tours on
the second battalion quadrangle. The cadet
received a certificate specifying that he was a
member of the most exclusive club on campus.
The document was signed and dated by The Boo.
Cadets eligible for the club, but overlooked by
The Boo, often came looking for him to receive
their certificate. One cadet wrote for his
certificate after his graduation.

★

When Boo was Tac of Band Company, he
initiated a Bum of the Year Award to be
presented to the most reprehensible private in
the senior class. Private Jones, Lehman, Vaux,

and Chamberlain wore this honor like a laurel wreath.

★

The Boo went through Third Battalion one day in 1968 on a casual search and destroy mission. He went in Ray Carpenter's room and opened a blue flight bag. A gin bottle was hidden under a sweater. There was a tablespoon of gin left in the bottle, The Boo let out a yell for the Officer of the Guard and told him to have Carpenter report to Jenkins Hall on the double. Carpenter came running before noon formation, swearing he thought the bottle was empty. In classic Courvoisie fashion, he bawled Carpenter out, threatened him with crucifixion and sent him out of the office with 25 confinements. Carpenter had the good sense to realize he was being let off the meat hook. To show Boo his heartfelt appreciation, he assembled the entire contingent of "I" Company on October 19 and serenaded The Boo with a spirited rendition of "Happy Birthday, Dear Boo."

★

Hal Mahar, drum major in Band Company, was baptized a Catholic in his senior year at The Citadel. The Boo and Mrs. Courvoisie attended the ceremony as godparents.

★

Bill Warner once crept up to The Boo's green Comet, raised the hood, placed a firecracker in the ignition system, closed the hood quietly, turned around to sneak back to his room, and bumped into The Boo who had watched the entire operation with keen interest.

The Father Who Traveled
The Hard Road

During the winter, The Boo shied away from any affiliation with the honor system. The danger always existed that the Commandant's Department could use the system as a weapon against the cadets, a practice which would seriously impair the effectiveness of the honor system itself. All the procedural affairs, such as the investigations and trials, were handled by the members of the honor court. But summer school was another matter entirely. No honor court remained on campus to pass judgment on peers who lied, cheated or stole during the sweltering months of June, July and August. As Colonel Courvoisie told Colonel James Carpenter, faculty advisor to the Honor Committee, "In the summer it is my baby. I have to write all the rules and the cadets have to play my kind of game. A cadet is a cadet whether it's winter or summer. If he is going to be honorable in January, then there is no reason why he should not be honorable in July. There is no one to enforce the honor system in the summer except me. It is my ball and glove."

So The Boo became a sort of one-man honor system. If someone was reported for stealing, The Boo would gather evidence, call the boy in, and give him two chances: he could either turn in his resignation as a cadet or stand trial for an honor violation when the Corps reconvened in September. In this way a continuity in the honor system was maintained throughout the year.

During the summer session of 1964 a boy was reported for stealing in the barracks. Boo investigated the case and accumulated the evidence from the cadets who turned the boy in. He then called the boy to his office. The boy admitted stealing the articles, but became terribly agitated and frightened when Colonel Courvoisie mentioned he would have to call his father to get permission to resign. In the course of the conversation, the boy told Boo that his father still beat him with his fists and that communication between them was almost non-existent except when the father screamed at him about his grades or beat him for some real or imagined offense. Why had the boy stolen? For no particular reason. His parents were wealthy. One of his sisters went to an exclusive school. He had no legitimate need to satisfy by stealing. His father sent him plenty of money. He had just stolen. That was that.

The father was born poor and raised in an ethnic ghetto on the West Side of Buffalo, New York. Life was a struggle from the very beginning, but by participating in life like a soldier in war, the father had struggled out of the bonds of poverty and made it big in the business world. He had crushed anyone who interfered with his rise. Ruthlessness and a certain reverence for the laws of survival had carried him past more compassionate men. He treated his family, and especially his only son, with the same hard nosed, tough-fisted attitude he used in his business. When he beat his son, it was because the boy had deviated from the path his father had predestined for him. No humor infected his conversation. Few smiles lit the darkness of his day or the somber tone of his mood. His family feared him. To the father this was as it should be.

The boy decided to go downtown to call his father. He drove slowly down King Street, unaware of the buildings he passed or the cars that passed him. His thoughts were riveted on the strange twist, the tragic turn his life had taken that day. He dreaded calling his father. He parked beside the Francis Marion Hotel, put a nickel into the parking meter, walked through the door and down to the basement level which had three pay telephone booths. He chose the middle one. The operator connected him with his father.

"Hello, Dad, I have something to tell you."

The Citadel had already informed him that his son had been caught stealing. He asked his son where he was calling from. The boy told him. The father then asked him to hold the line for one moment while he tended to some business that could not wait. The boy waited for over five minutes. His father then came back on the phone and bawled his son out savagely for the next five minutes. The tongue lashing would have continued interminably it seemed, until the boy looked up and saw a policeman staring at him. The policeman opened the door and said, "Son, we got a call from your father five minutes ago. He wants us to keep an eye on you until he can get to Charleston."

The boy heard a click on the other end of the receiver.

The Boo received a call about three o'clock that afternoon from the Chief of Police. He told The Boo about the phone call from Buffalo and the subsequent jailing of the boy until his father's arrival. By three-thirty The Boo stood outside of a crowded cell, staring at the boy behind bars. The Charleston jail is a snake-pit in the summertime. The oppressive heat in the dank, moist cells that overlook the Cooper River makes breathing strenuous work. Thieves and drunks lie in dark corners, sometimes silent, at other times muttering curses to themselves or anyone willing to listen.

"This is no damn place for a boy to be, and you know it," The Boo told the Chief of Police.

"I know that, Colonel, but what can I do about it?"

"If I take the responsibility for the boy and promise that he will be waiting when his father gets here, will you let him go then?"

"Sure, Colonel, if I have your word."

"You've got it."

As Boo looked into the cell, the boy lifted his head and greeted him. Sweat poured off the boy's face.

"Bubba, you can come home with me if you promise not to run off."

"Thanks anyway, Colonel, but I'll stick it out here."

The Boo left but returned two hours later and repeated his offer. This time the boy said, "Yes, Colonel, I'll be glad to come home with you."

Since the boy's mother and father were

driving from Buffalo and would not arrive in Charleston until later the next night, Colonel and Mrs. Courvoisie gave him the run of the house, showed him the refrigerator, told him to raid it when hungry, and allowed him to come and go from the house and campus as he pleased. He had pledged his word to the Colonel that he would not try to leave. He watched television the first evening until eleven o'clock and then after saying good night, slept in the bed in Al's bedroom.

The next afternoon, the Courvoisie family went to Hampton to watch Bishop England's football team scrimmage Hampton High School. Al Courvoisie anchored the right side of Bishop England's offensive line at the tackle position. They told their house guest they would return at about eight in the evening. The boy left before they did to see a tennis match across the street. When the Courvoisies left for Hampton, they forgot to lift the latch which unlocked the front door.

After the scrimmage which saw Bishop England trounce the Red Devils in a highly competitive contest, the Courvoisies returned to Charleston. As they pulled into their back yard, the headlights of the car swung around to the back steps where they saw the motionless figure of the boy sitting. He had been there for four hours.

It embarrassed the hell out of both Colonel and Mrs. Courvoisie.

"I wanted to be here when you got back, Colonel. I didn't want you to think I slipped out on you."

After profuse apologies were offered and

accepted, Mrs. Courvoisie prepared a dinner of hamburgers and french fries with chocolate cake and lime sherbet for dessert. There was much laughter and the boy seemed to loosen up in the warm atmosphere of the Courvoisie dining table. At nine-thirty, his parents arrived at the front door.

Mrs. Courvoisie went to the door. Before her stood a small, meek woman whose eyes reflected the fear of one who had been beaten down by a more powerful presence. Next to her was the boy's father, thin and powerfully built, with a scowling face and lean, hard body that reminded one of an experienced pugilist.

"Good evening, won't you come in?" Mrs. Courvoisie asked.

"Where's my boy? He's supposed to be here," the father answered.

"He's here," Mrs. Courvoisie retorted.

The boy's parents walked into the room and stood facing their son. They did not speak to him, only stared at him.

Finally the boy said, "My things are upstairs, I'll go get them."

The father flared and said much too loudly, "You knew we were coming, why in the hell didn't you have the stuff ready?"

"I don't know, Dad."

"We drove all the way from Buffalo and you're not even ready. Do you think we enjoyed the trip?"

"Well, your son has been a big help around the house," Mrs. Courvoisie said as the boy went upstairs to collect his things. "He's dried the dishes and made up his bed. He even offered to clean the basin in the bathroom."

This was met with complete silence, neither parent signifying that they had even heard what she said. Colonel Courvoisie was upstairs reading the paper when they had first come in. He now was coming down the stairs.

"I think the Colonel wants to talk to you," Mrs. Courvoisie said.

"And I sure have some things to say to him," the father answered venomously.

Normally The Boo handles parents gingerly, a charmer who relies on basic military etiquette to win the hearts and souls of people who know him by name and reputation from hearing their sons talk. Normally, that is.

On this particular night the trappings of the gentleman fell to the floor. Boo had heard the conversation which took place before he came down. He was not smiling as he descended the stairs. For the first and last time he did not shake hands with a parent who stood before him. The two men glared at each other. The room fell silent. Finally The Boo spoke.

"My name's Courvoisie."

"I know who you are," the man answered.

"Don't be hard on the boy. He made a mistake," Boo continued.

"You're damn right he made a mistake. He'll pay for it, too."

"Mr., I'm going to tell you something. You've got a good boy. It's about time you started supporting your son instead of knocking the hell out of him every time he turns around. Start showing him you love him. Let him know you love him no matter what he does. Don't make a horse's ass out of yourself and your son just because he made one mistake. Start being a father to your boy here. Quit your growling and your cursing and start showing some love, Mister."

Boo's face went red. He did nothing to hide or restrain his anger. Both men stared at each other with hard, uncompromising stares. The power of Boo's monologue hung suspended in the quiet of the room. The two men eyeballed each other. Neither of them spoke.

As the boy started to carry his luggage out to the car Mrs. Courvoisie went up and kissed him on the cheek. "Whenever you come back to Charleston, you can always stay with us," she said.

"Good luck, Bubba. Let me know how everything turns out. You'll be all right. Things have a way of working out," The Boo added.

"Thanks very much, Colonel. Thank you, Mrs. Courvoisie, thanks a lot."

He went through the door first. His mother, who had not spoken a single word, followed. His father started out, looked back at the Colonel, said nothing and walked into the night.

The Moon Shot

Friday morning. Day before graduation. The beauty of the military college burgeons each year on this very special day, filled with the show and splendor of the final parades, the award ceremonies, the pomp and circumstance of the military in the act of performing its art for thousands of enthusiastic visitors. Colonel Duckett was riding down East Bay Street early Friday morning. The imposing homes of the Battery swept past him unnoticed; his mind was riveted on the morning's activities in which he always played a major and important part. A car driven by two cadets swerved past him and pulled along side of a car in front of him. One of the cadets pulled down his pants and flashed his naked behind to the driver of the other vehicle. Colonel Duckett took the car's license number.

Colonel Courvoisie found the car on his first swing of the campus. It had no Citadel sticker. He went into the O.C.'s room in No. Two Barracks and put a call through to the motor vehicle department in Columbia. A parade was just ending. The Boo went to first battalion to await the arrival of the cadet's company. It came. Squads of cadets in perfect formation walked to the monotonous voice of the drums, when the voice of Boo called the cadet's name loud enough for the gods to hear. This was one of The Boo's most formidable weapons. To be called from the middle of a company of marching cadets, to go from a single component, nameless and anonymous, in one moment, to a special doomed name roared from the foghorn voice of Colonel Courvoisie, had psychological implications that were devastating. The boy came out.

"Who was with you, Bubba?"

In five minutes, an ERW sat before General Clark, "Driving a car—Indecent Exposure."

The driver received 10/120. Colonel Courvoisie had to call the other boy's parents to give him permission to resign. On this particular day, when The Boo called, the father broke down and wept uncontrollably.

As The Boo said later, "There isn't any fun in that. It's like saying, 'Sir, put this in writing: Send your son to the bottom most pit of hell and tell him to stay there the rest of his life.'"

The Great Cedar

Every year before Christmas furlough, the freshmen go into the woods around Charleston in search of the largest, finest Christmas tree in the area. Each company displays this tree proudly in its company area. It was natural that a feeling of competition infected each company about the size and grandeur of their tree. A great amount of pressure fell on the heads of young freshmen who often failed to understand the strange and misplaced Christmas spirit of their elders. But the word of upperclassmen was law and each year the freshmen entered into the war of Christmas tree with great vigor.

In December of 1964, the harried knobs of "N" Company scrambled around the woods near Moncks Corner looking for a tree which would satisfy the finicky corporals who were making their lives miserable. They finally found a tree which looked big enough. Several axes went to work, and in twenty minutes the tree chosen to represent "N" Company before God and man plummeted to the earth. The knobs shouted, dragged the tree to the truck they had rented for the occasion and drove it back to The Citadel. They were the last company in Fourth Battalion to erect their tree. When they did, laughter broke out all over the barracks. The "N" Company tree looked like a midget in a field of giants. The tree which had looked so large in the forest looked bent and misshapen compared to the other trees in Fourth Battalion. The embarrassed corporals of "N" Company organized a spontaneous sweat party. Afterwards, they sent the angry freshmen out to find another tree.

They searched all over Charleston county. They scoured the back roads. They covered every inch of forest they cou. l find. Finally, they found it. The tree towered skyward for fifty feet or more. It was a gigantic cedar tree, beautifully proportioned and magnificently straight. It took as much engineering skill to get the tree back to The Citadel as it took for Egyptian slaves to lift the blocks of granite for the pyramids. But they did it. When the tree was finally up, it was twice as big as any other tree in the regiment. Isaac Metts, the Company Commander, was ecstatic. Bill Gordon, the First Sergeant, was overjoyed. Even the vulpine staff of corporals could barely contain their delight. No tree at The Citadel could match it.

The next day a heart-rending picture graced the front page of the Charleston *News and Courier*. A man stood with a glum face beside a huge, jagged tree stump. The accompanying article told of a cedar tree the man had planted in his youth. He planted the tree when he was eight years old and had measured his passage on the earth by its growth. He was proud of his tree. He loved the tree. He wept when he walked out of his house and found the tree's towering presence gone from the horizon. Someone had come on his property and cut the tree down without his permission. He had notified the Charleston police and they were looking for the culprits.

Word spread slowly. But soon cadets were coming out of their rooms and looking at the tree by "N" Company. They held copies of the newspaper in their hands. They looked at the tree. Then they looked at the old man and the stump. Then they looked at the tree again. .

Isaac Metts came to The Boo's home that afternoon. "Colonel Courvoisie, how would you like a nice big pile of cedar for your fireplace?"

"What's wrong, Bubba?" The Boo asked.

Metts answered, "Colonel, do you know that tree every cop in Charleston is looking for?"

"You mean the old man's tree that was in the paper this morning?"

"You've got the one, Colonel. Well, we got it. Or at least we had it. It's now chopped up into a million little pieces of firewood. Colonel, we need a place to put it," Metts pleaded.

"Bring it to my garage, Bubba. We can store it in there until we figure out what in the hell to do with it."

The cedar filled the whole garage. Boo called the Chief of Police and explained the traditional hunt for the largest Christmas tree. Things were smoothed over. Metts and the freshmen had to go to General Clark's office and apologize to the old man. Christmas came as usual that year.

More ERW's

14 April 1966

SUBJECT: Explanation of Report: "Absent Muster, 12 April," D/L 13 April 1966

TO: The Commandant of Cadets.

1. The report is correct.

2. Upon arriving home Easter morning I removed my false teeth and placed them on my dresser. My dog, Cindy, being her mischievous self snuffed out my teeth. She must have mistaken them for candy, because she gnawed them until they were completely destroyed. When waking up Easter morning I realized my dog's wrong doing and I realized that she did know what she had done. No punishment was applied. Monday I made an appointment to have my teeth repaired. The earliest possible date to have them repaired was Tuesday. I telephoned the authorities at The Citadel and notified them that I would be late returning. Because of the lack of speed of the Greyhound, I was later than anticipated returning to school. Because of my dog's lack of intelligence, but keen sense of smell, my teeth were destroyed. Because of my dog's inabilities and abilites, I am at your mercy for minimum punishment.

3. The offense was intentional.

★

3 March 1966

SUBJECT: Explanation of Report: "Improper
            Drill Report, February 25, 1966,"
            D/L March 1966
TO: The Commandant of Cadets

1. The report is correct.

2. The offense stated above is correct. I did perform with human frailty an error by placing Cadet Fisher's name on the report twice. In our lowly lives upon this earth men at times have made errors of even more grievous nature. I ask no pity for my dire offense but would cite St. Matthew 5:7, "Blessed are the merciful: for they shall obtain mercy."

As to the second part of my offense I would say that Cadet Witt's name was omitted from my list of the Corps Squad through an unintentional oversight. I could not hold the Squad Leader or his Assistant liable for such a deed. Therefore, on the second count I shall plead guilty, not ask for clemency, and march forthwith to the guillotine with my loyal and stalwart Supply Sergeant who at this time also is submitting an explanation of a similar report.

3. The offense was unintentional.

                    1st   Sgt.   of   Humblest
Stature, Co. A
                    2nd Class

★

19 May 1966

SUBJECT: Explanation of Report: "Absent
            Chemistry, 2nd Offense, 11 May
            1966," D/L 18 May 1966.

TO: The Commandant of Cadets.

1. The report is correct.
2. At *ten fifteen* I opened my eyes,
   And when fully awake I realized
   That *another* chemistry class was missed.
   I was again in sinful abyss.

   The *dirty old man?* caught me dead to
      rights.
   No twisting nor turning can save me from
      this.
   Upon his good mercy, I place myself,
   For that 9 o'clock chem class that I missed.

   Now none can complain about this verse,
   Which is much better than the first.
   So how about ten merits for me,
   For exceptionally outstanding poetry.
3. The offense was unintentional.

                              29 November 1963

SUBJECT: Explanation of Report: "Walking
            around library with shoes off, 17
            November," D/L 27 November
TO: The Commandant of Cadets.

1. The report is correct.
2. Colonel Courvoisie had taken my boots
away from me, leaving me to face the world
bootless. To prevent holes being worn in my
socks, I borrowed a pair of shoes until mine
arrived in the mail. Much to my dismay,
however, the shoes were just a tad too tight. It is
a common fact that a student will study better
when he is comfortable than otherwise. As the

shoes were wearing blisters on my heels and pinching my toes, I was literally forced to remove the inflictors of pain. During my process of acquiring scholarly knowledge, my throat began to run rampant with thirst. Not wishing to be seen walking around the library in my stocking feet, I tiptoed my way behind the book shelves but alas, my plot was foiled by Mr. Stiger. If you have no mercy on me, have mercy on my feet.

3. The offense was unintentional.

★

May 12, 1966

SUBJECT: Explanation of Report: "Late L,"
            05/08/66, D/L 05/11/66
TO: The Commandant of Cadets

1. The report is correct.

2. On the date of said offense while returning from a weekend leave, as a rider with Cadet M. Foster, a few miles out of Charleston we came upon a woman beside Interstate 26 with a flat tire. Being the gentlemen and scholars that Citadel men are, Cadet Foster and I (naturally exemplifying these qualities) stopped and assisted the distressed woman by changing her tire for her. As we were bringing credit upon the school through our valorous actions we were unfortunately late returning from leave. Such actions as these are *meritorious* deeds rather than punishable deeds.

3. The offense was unintentional.

★

19 May 1966

SUBJECT: Explanation of Report: "Flying
            kite from top gallery,"
            D/L 18 March 1964.
TO: The Commandant of Cadets.

1. The report is correct.
2. I have searched *The Blue Book*
   through and through,
   And never has it been read so true,
   And nowhere could I site
   Anything against me flying a kite.
   Young Ben Franklin was not "pulled" that
     night,
   And neither were Orville or Wilbur Wright
   Spring is here and we're feeling light,
   So don't keep us in for flying a kite.
3. There is thought to be no offense com-
mitted.

★

17 March 1964

SUBJECT: Reconsideration of Award:
            "Late to Class, 12 March
            1964," D/L 13 March 1964.
TO: The Commandant of Cadets.

1. The report is correct.
2. It is true I was late, upon that date,
   But the teacher was later than I,
   And since your demerits decide my fate,
   Remove them, and let it go by.

   He was later than me, by a minute you see,
   Which I know was not proper for him,

So if you are as kind, as I know you can be,
You'll free me and give them to him.

3. The offense was unintentional.

★

23 March 1964

SUBJECT: Explanation of Report: "Throwing
            food in the mess hall, 12 March
            1964," D/L 21 March 1964.

TO: The Commandant of Cadets.

1. The report is correct.
2. I'm afraid that you have caught me "dead
to rights" and I have no excuse. However, being
a Political Science major, I plead self-defense
because I was fired upon first.
3. The offense was done in self-defense.

★

4 May 1964

SUBJECT: Reconsideration of Award:
            "Visiting hospital during off
            hours without signing out
            guardroom, 24 April,"
            D/L 1 May.

TO: The Commandant of Cadets

1. The report is correct.
2. On this occasion I was carried to the
hospital on a litter and could not sign out in the
guardroom.
3. The offense was unintentional.

★

16 January 1964

SUBJECT: Explanation of Report: "Absent D
           I," D/L 14 January 1964
TO: The Commandant of Cadets.

1. The report is a little demoralizing but
correct.

2. Upon entering my 5th year of attendance
at this institution, I have considered The Citadel
as my home. Certainly it cannot be denied that
longevity has made me feel like a long-standing
member of this institution.

My striving ambition is to become a real
senior and graduate someday. As stated in the
1963-64 *Guidon*, page 6, paragraph 3 . . . "The
Citadel is a college for th poor boy, wealthy
boy, for the ambitious b_ who will rule his
spirit. . . ." and in an attempt to raise my spirits
one last time before the oncoming exams, I took
advantage of senior leave on 11 January when
my morale was at an all time low.

I sincerely hope that my ambitions will not be
menaced by a hasty reinforcement of my psychological fear, "confinsophobia" (Latin for
fear of confinements) and that the proper
therapy will be employed so that I may become
a useful member of society; i.e., that is 5
demerits.

3. The offense was intentional.

★

22 March 1963

SUBJECT: Explanation of Report: "Reporting
to Mess Hall individually,
12 March 1965," D/L 19 March
1965.

TO: The Commandant of Cadets.

1. The report is correct.
2. On the date of the infraction
    My mind was in traction;
Because this afternoon there had been
    inspection,
For which I had shined up to perfection.

Then came a parade, with all its show
That made my skull work real, real slow;
It put my body under control of my rack
Which after this bliss, pulled me in the
    sack.

I awoke as the troops were marching to
    mess
And with thoughts of suckulant food,
    started to dress;
I hurried, only a little bit late, to Coward
    Hall
Only to find that I shouldn't have gone at
    all.
3. The offense was intentional.

★

3 May 1966

SUBJECT: Explanation of Report: "Absent
Social-Intellectual History,
26 April 1966," D/L 2 May 1966.

TO: The Commandant of Cadets.

1. The report is correct.

2. In Spring when the world is mudluscious
    My thoughts wander far and free.
O Society and Intellectual History
    Your call is deaf to me.
When sea gulls' calls are lifted
    O'r Charleston garbage dumps,
I find myself emerged
    In absorbing history lumps.
Spring's call is wild and delicious
    I must not tarry here,
But wander about the Cid Campus
    Where its sound is music on my ear.
A poet is true I may not be,
    but I humbly impore they pity
On your lamb in agony
Though four walls do not a prison make,
    And Spring's glad son invades the
    harshes
       prison walls
I accept my fate though big or small.

3. The offense was intentional.

★

2 March 1965

SUBJECT: Explanation of Report: "Animals
           in Room 2nd Offense 23 February,"
           D/L 1 March.
TO: The Commandant of Cadets.

1. The report is correct.
2. On the 15th of February the animals

(species Hamstro) were returned to room 1307. We assumed that this was an indication that they were not to establish a permanent residency in the Commandant's Department. At this time our concern was two fold.

1st. That the Hamstros be properly taken care of since the health of the two species was in a condition of pregnancy. We were concerned with the present condition of the Hamstros because we felt we owed an obligation to the species of properly caring for them since the status of pregnancy occurred while they were boarders in our company headquarters. Moving the species at that time would have meant possible physical damage.

2nd. We had good intentions of removing the species as soon as the present period of hardship was terminated. Since it was obvious that the Commandant's Department felt such companionship was unwarranted we would have immediately carried out these wishes if it had not been for the above status of the Hamstros.

To further substantiate our actions we regret to announce the death of the two Hamstros referred to above. They passed on after discovery of their habitat for the second time. We wasted no time in removing the Hamstros from "B" Company's area, this move resulted in the mentioned death of the referred Hamstros.

In conclusion, we were guided by the principle of discretion in the interest of humanity and maintenance of Headquarters morale.

3. The offense was intentional.

★

14 April 66

SUBJECT: Explanation of Report:
           "Throwing food in mess hall
           04/01/66." D/L 04/13/66.
TO: The Commandant of Cadets

   1. The report is correct.

   2. On the date of the aforementioned offense, I noticed a classmate greedily trying to protect an exceptionally large piece of chocolate cream pie. With the joyness of Friday and the chicanery of April Fool's, I made mock attempts to pilfer the pie. On one attempt, I bumped the defender, causing his hand to strike the pie. Perceiving a messy reprisal, I made a futile attempt to flee. While this classmate was cleaning his hand on my shoulder, Mr. Reeves was inadvertently splattered. Admitting these actions were a misdemeanor, I contend that there was no harmful or dangerous throwing of food, but merely a bit of smearing.

   3. The offense was unintentional.

★

SUBJECT: "Assuming of Upper-Class
           Privilege 19 January, 1966,"
           D/L January, 1966.
TO: The Commandant of Cadets.

   1. The report is correct.

   2. The day in question was last Friday, when drill and parade were rained out. The upper-classmen of third battalion, to celebrate their

jubilation, were playing catch from gallery to gallery, trans quadrangle. There were numerous misses and the balls fell to the quad. Paying tribute to their class and position here at The Citadel, and at the same time trying to win their favor, I, like an humble dog, retrieved their balls. I am sure that at no time did I penetrate the depths of the hallowed quad more than fifteen feet. For this devout loyalty and servitude I was rewarded unjustly with an E.R.W.

3. The offense was unintentional.

★

SUBJECT: Explanation of Report: "Absent March to Stadium, 8 October 1966," D/L 14 October 1966.
TO: The Commandant of Cadets.

1. The report is correct.

2. On the date of the report, I went to Mess, where, in the typical pre-game tension and excitement displayed by the Corps, I was bombarded by various and sundry delectable morsels from our choice menu. Since I did not choose to go to the game smelling like a tuna-fish sandwich or looking like a baked bean, I took a shower and dressed in a clean uniform. When I stepped out of my room:

"what to my wondering eyes should appear,
    an empty quad, they had left me here."

I proceeded to the game under my own (clean) steam and was there in time for the "daring dash" to the stands.

3. The offense was unintentional.

★

SUBJECT: Explanation of Report:
"Improper Uniform on Campus,
9 December 1966," D/L 12
December, 1966.

TO: The Commandant of Cadets

1. The report is correct.

2. In the course of events of all men's lives, there falls an occasional pestilence of ill which plagues the happiness and security of all ensconced in a particular community. So it has been with us at The Citadel. A thief has come into our midst, and he has created a schism amidst the bounds of brotherhood around our campus conclave in the form of mutual mistrust.

On Friday the ninth of December, Cadet James A. Probsdorfer sorrowfully brought the aforementioned weighty matter before The Corps of Cadets at the conclusion of our noon meal. He discussed the gravity of the blight, and he required everyone to be especially watchful lest the thief survive to afflict us further. Friday was a day of natural beauty and warmth, but as the cadet corps streamed from the mess hall, there was no correlation between the shining sun and downtrodden looks of faces forlorn. There was none of the levity which usually precedes a forthcoming weekend, and comraderie was non-extant.

I felt that such a state of lethargy with every soul lost deep in the "slough of dispond," as

John Bunyan's *Pilgrim's Progress* described it, was an unhealthy state in which to leave our student body. Donning, in addition to my regular mixed-field uniform, a garrison cap, chin-strap turned up so as to emulate a Hell's Angel, a white handkerchief over my face in the manner of Billy the Kid, and a pair of black fingerprint-proof gloves, and, placing a lock box under my arm, I set out to raise the Corp's morale.

I went first to the room of our battalion honor representative. My ludicrous appearance then left the battalion commander and his exec in a fit of great hilarity. Venturing toward the second battalion, and after receiving the cheers of the cadet contingent present, I made my way to our Regimental Commander's room, in which my appearance broke the heavy air and was received with warm amusement. Entering the third battalion and feeling highly gratified by the effort of my presence there, I struck upon the idea of holding-up Major Brand, in mock. Having achieved this design with paramount success, I was heading back to my room when I was upended by Captain Motley.

Captain Motley, drawn up in Ozimandian anger, inquired as to my intent. I assured him that my disguise was one of levity, rather than being an attempt to disguise or deceive. However, he did not understand, and the report which may be read above was entered.

3. The offense was, for the best of all, intentional.

★

SUBJECT: Explanation of Report: "Wrong
           way on one way street, 04/16/67"
           D/L 04/19/67
TO: The Commandant of Cadets.

1. The report is absolutely and unequivocally incorrect.

2. My suggestions as to the manner in which the reporting officer should execute his responsibility is far from acceptable here. I do however feel, regardless of the bitterness resulting from failure to keep a cadet in until graduation, he should not report a cadet who was not even driving for going the wrong way on a street, which as a mere aside was not even done by the driver of the car. Mere assumptions will not stand up in a court of law, even though they may stand in your court. On the other hand if it was a mere optical fantasy created by . . . poor sight . . . old age . . . spite . . . senility, then I suggest consulting the closest attache of Medicare.

3. Since the report is incorrect, it obviously was intentional.

★

SUBJECT: Explanation of Report: "On
           Barracks Roof Unauth, 19 April
           1967,"
           D/L dated 21 April 1967.
TO: The Commandant of Cadets

1. The report is correct.

2. I was blown up there by a sudden gust of wind and while up there I decided to check it out for suitability for a Senior Class Party.

3. As you can see, the offense was unintentional if there was any offense at all.

★

SUBJECT: Explanation of Report: "Late
              W E L, 5 March 1967, D/L 8 March
              1967.
TO: The Commandant of Cadets.

1. The report is correct.

2. That screaming clock makes my blood run
        cold.
   Gabriels trump! The big bull elephant
   Squeals "Late" to the parched herd. The
        lambs bleat
   And jabber that it's speed they want.

   Within my blood my ancient kindred
        spoke,-
   Grotesque and monstrous voices, heard
        afar
   You cannot leave a friend wishing to
        revoke
   His loved ones and home for The Citadel
        star.

   And suddenly, as in a flash of light,
   I saw great nature working out her plan.
   She called for care from mastadon to mite,
   "Safe driving;" Chevy speed groped thru
        the night.

   On that long road we came to seek
        mankind;
   Here were the darling converts penitent
        home

Circumstance upheld us into sin quite
   blind.
And you are left to judge us from your
   dome.

3. The offense was unintentional.

SUBJECT: Explanation of Report: "late
           R W E L, 4 March 1968,"
           D/L 6 March 1968.
TO: The Commandant of Cadets.

1. The report is correct.

2. Upon returning from a long weekend my
car had internal troubles in Jacksonville,
Florida. Being the good-guy that I am I
immediately looked for a hospital to take it to.
The only one available, being that it was a
Sunday afternoon, was Obi's Hospital (alias
"Obi's 24 Hour Garage") run by Ed L. Obi,
President. He put the car on the rack and after a
few minutes I met its doctor. He was Sonny the
Executive Vice President of Obi's. He had
degrees of all kind. First was a degree from
Boondock Mechanics School, next was a
diploma from Hicksville Transmission Repair.
Ed Obi came in and gave his diagnosis and said
he would have to operate. The operation lasted
20 hours. Being the great doctor he is, Sonny
made the patient recover in record time. Upon
the speedy recovery we thanked Ed Obi and his
assistant and chief resident Sonny and
proceeded on our journey.

★

SUBJECT: Reconsideration of Awards:
           "Gross Personal Appearance on
           Campus, 16 Nov.," D/L Nov.
           29, 1967.

TO: The Commandant of Cadets

1. The report is correct.

2. When I read the D/L bearing the damnable
report of above, I was filled with shock and
disbelief. Not only was I charged of being in
gross attire while on campus, but it also seemed
that I was the one who had reported me.
Regaining my composure, I felt that the only
sensible thing to do was to sit down and ask
myself why I had pulled me. During the course
of the discussion I found out many interesting
things. I found that I was in a state of undue
excitement when I entered the report.
Apparently I had no idea of what I was doing at
the time. This seemed like a logical explanation
to me. I also found that I considered myself a
rather chic dresser, despite my somewhat
limited wardrobe. Kind of the Beau Brummel of
the Cadet Set. At any rate, both of us, or should
I say both of me, decided that the report was a
terrible mistake and that I should be showered
with merits for my rather astute dressing
habits.

★

TO: Commandant

1. Explanation of Report: D/L 3 Dec. 1965,
"Absent Parade 11/20/65."

a. Report is incorrect.

b. It is a dirty lie aimed at slandering my good name and reputation.

c. There was no offense.

★

SUBJECT: Explanation of Report: "Being
           Too Thin, 9 December,"
           D/L 10 December.

TO: The Commandant of Cadets.

1. The report is correct.

2. The skeletal structure of my body is located too close to the surface of my skin, and, therefore, I appear to be undernourished. However, measures have been initiated to correct the situation.

3. The offense was unintentional.

★

TO: The Commandant of Cadets.

1. The report is believed to be correct.

2. The excitement, tension, pressure and pain of the two days just prior to the 26th of February had caused the ratio of gastric acid to all the necessary and abundant materials in my stomach to sky rocket. This completely abnormal ratio plus the Sunday Special of Coward Hall mixed in with a time factor equaled one thing—the latrine. It just so happened that the solution came out at the same time confinements began. This unfortunate incident caused a momentary delay in reporting for confinements.

3. The offense was caused by "Mother Nature."

★

SUBJECT: Reconsideration of Award:
           "Telephone ESP, 5 October,"
           D/L 7 October.
TO: The Commandant of Cadets

1. Alas, I am guilty.

2. On the fateful day in question my dearly beloved called me from many miles away (long distance) and the fateful hour of 2000 (8:00 P.M.) was the only time in which she could successfully reach me, although she had been trying to contact me for many hours that infamous day. She had the heartbreaking task of informing me that this weekend, the one in which both of us were anxiously awaiting, would be just another weekend since she could not come down. Surely the gods that be must realize that this alone is enough and perhaps more punishment then any mere, humble, mortal can endure.

3. The offense was unintentional.

★

SUBJECT: Explanation of Report: "MRI
           Too Much Hair 12 January,"
           D/L 14 January.
TO: The Commandant of Cadets.

1. The report is correct.
2. While standing at formation
   They called a noon inspection
   When they stepped in front of me
   All that they could see
   Was a curl that did flap

From beneath my little cap.
He shuddered and he snorted
And his face became distorted.
It was all that I could bear
To be pulled for too much hair.
3. There was no violation.

★

SUBJECT: Explanation of Report: "Throwing
            food in Mess Hall, 4/1/66,"
            D/L 4/1/66.
TO: The Commandant of Cadets.

1. The report is correct.
2. The incident occurred during the noon
meal on a Friday. We had chocolate cream pie
for desert. I was standing by my chair joking
with a friend about splattering him with my pie,
which I was holding in my hand. Another of my
friends came up to me. We began bumping each
other, both being filled with the feeling of jollity
which is only present on Friday. My hand was
bumped into my pie. In retribution, I turned to
wipe my hand, which by this time was filled
with the remnants of my delicious chocolate
cream pie, on the back of my bumptious friend.
My friend, unfortunately, had begun to run
away. Thus my wipe was correctly an extended
swipe. Another friend was splattered in the
holocaust, and he also being of a revengeful
nature, wiped his share of my cream pie on my
unsuspecting and defenseless clean gray shirt.
Approximately fifteen minutes had passed
when, to my surprise, the O.C. appeared in that

hallowed area of the mess hall which seats Company T. He expressed his displeasure at the childish pie-burst, and asked that the sinners describe their damnable actions to him in writing. This I have done. I close with the hope that the reader of this epistle will stop for a minute, imagine himself a humble cadet for a moment, and realize that a cadet on Friday feels joy which is often uncontrollable, but which joy is nevertheless, thanks to the cadet's iron will, channeled into such harmless diversions as the inadvertent wiping of chocolate cream pie.

3. The offense was unintentional.

★

SUBJECT: Explanation of Report: "Sitting with girl in East Stand," 12 Nov. 66.

TO: The Commandant of Cadets

1. The report is correct.

2. We, my date and I, arrived at the scene of the gridiron classic (Johnson Hagood Stadium), early in the afternoon and long before the opening kickoff. Unfortunately, she was feeling rather poorly (possibly a consequence of the preceding meal in Coward Hall?) and we unfortunately were forced to sit directly in front of several senior Cadets who sported airhorns, klaxon horns, and an assortment of cow bells. We sat in this locale throughout the first half, and possibly our choice of seats resulted in my date's subsequent headache and periodic chills. She pleaded that we move away or leave the contest entirely. As a compromise

measure, and an effort to remain a gentlemen
and a cadet, I offered to take her into the sun
and away from the noise. The only area where
both of these factors existed was the East
Stand. We crossed the gridiron while the
Summerall Guards were forming up, and
proceeded with haste to Section M. Located in
that section was a school acquaintance, another
female by the name of Patricia MacClemests.
She was dating a "knob" from Band Company,
and sitting with the knob's parents. Throughout
the half time entertainment, my date showed
signs of improvement. But as the second half
began, she was still not ready to suffer the
torture of our senior date section seats. The
game began and due to her state, I did not feel it
wise to bring her back across the field as she
may have gotten hurt in the end zone area as the
Dogs seemed to occupy the area quite
frequently. The other factor was that of the
unknown. Were our seats still empty or had
they been usurped? This then was why in a rare
display of Cadet chivalry, I placed the well
being of my date above the monumental
consequence of the just and omnipotent
Assistant Commandant.

3. The offense was not intentional, but it
was an act of mercy sparing my date for
unnecessary suffering. I rest my case.

★

SUBJECT: Reconsideration of Award (No
            Front Sticker 16, 17, 18, 19, 20, 21,
            22 March 1964, D/L 23 March 1964)
TO: The Commandant of Cadets.

1. The report is correct.

2. There are and always have been Citadel stickers on my car. However, on the date of the report my front sticker was probably covered with an advertisement sticker. Several days before the report was entered, as a practical joke someone put 10 or 12 stickers on my windows, bumpers, hood, etc. of my car. I took the stickers off as soon as I discovered them but since there were so many, I must have neglected to see the one covering my front Citadel sticker. Now, as a result of the report and the shock of seeing 40 demerits in conjunction with my name, I have removed that sticker which covered my front Citadel sticker. Both of my Citadel stickers are now clearly visible and readable at a distance. As proof of this, I submit the following photographs taken on March 24 at 1130 hours at a distance of 300 feet from my car. The first photograph was enlarged four times and the second one approximately thirty times. As evident from the second photograph, my number 64-125 is clearly readable to the average man with good vision.

3. The offense was unintentional.

★

SUBJECT: Explanation of Report: "Absent
            Fire Drill, 24 Oct.,"
            D/L Oct. 27, 1967.
TO: The Commandant of Cadets

1. The report is correct.

2. I was on fourth division fighting the consuming flames of exhaustion.

★

Punishment Order No. 54

PUNISHMENT ORDER

1. For "Returning General Leave in Civilian Clothes, 1 October": Cadet Courvoisie, A. Company A, 3rd Class.

10 Demerits
20 Tours

A. The attention of Cadet Courvoisie, A., Company A, 3rd Class is directed to sub-paragraph 430a, *The Blue Book* 1966, which applies in this case.

By Command of Major General Tucker:
     (handwritten) With love

> T. N. Courvoisie,
> Lt. Colonel, U.S.A.
> Ret'd., Assistant
> Commandant of
> Cadets.

Me and The Boo

I just missed being selected regimental commander my senior year at The Citadel. Only five hundred cadets had a better chance of being chosen. Jim Probsdorfer, a glittering example of military virtue, edged me out in a fiercely contested battle. To help soothe my ruffled feathers, I was offered a position of command and responsiblity as a senior private in the third squad, second platoon of Romeo Company. I accepted the job with the poker face and jutting jaw of the defeated soldier.

From the very beginning of my tenture at The Citadel, I never qualified in anyone's mind as a model cadet. Nor did anyone prophesy that my name would one day be compared to Hannibal's or Napoleon's in discussions about military strategists. I never learned to clean a rifle, never cured the odd, bouncing walk that cost "R" Company several parades, and never felt comfortable in the uniform other cadets wore like a pelt. The shock of "hell night," when I stood terrified before the onslaught of a world gone mad, when the cadre shrieked and brutalized the eight squads of freshmen offered to them, never left me. To see plebe after plebe fall to the quadrangle, sweating hideously, unconscious and numb, bothered my frail sensibilities. To see arms go limp from pushups, legs grow useless from running in place, and voices grow hoarse from screaming puzzled me. To see the hooked noses and bloodshot eyes of upperclassmen pressed against my face, their fetid breath hot against my neck and ears, their mouths cruel and twisted beneath the glare of the barracks lights, terrified me. The shock of this one long night of tolerated sadism ended any love affair I might have had with the plebe system. My goal in life from that moment was to somehow escape from being sucked into the delusion that screaming lunatics with stripes on their shoulders and bars on their hats were even remotely connected with leadership. Nor did I believe the confines of the fourth battalion represented the world as it was or as it should be. My Citadelian personality was forged on the second night of my college career when after an hour of intense, magnified racking, a bugle blew mercifully and I took one step toward my room, fell to my knees, crawled to my bed, and spent a sleepless night wondering how the fates had plotted against me and how in God's name the furies had managed to bring me under this vindictive jurisdiction.

It was a hell of a beginning, but traumatic enough to force me to develop theories of survival which were to serve me well until the day of my graduation. The 720-day theory of grayness was my first project. The color gray dominated the entire landscape of the college. Gray walls, gray uniforms, gray buildings, gray food in the mess hall, gray expressions on the faces of antiquated professors who delivered gray lectures in cobweb voices—the grayness of concealment became the clothing I assumed, and with this weapon I was able to pass through the portals of Lesesne Gate with remarkable unremarkability. I blended in, assumed a cloak of anonymity, tried to straddle the line beside the abyss, and hoped to escape the scarred outlook I saw daily in the faces of young men who had already been through the system.

I stayed away from The Boo. I have already described the initial moment his voice rent the harmony and comradery of the Isle of Palms outing. As administrator of discipline and grand inquisitor for the Commandant's Department, I reasoned there was no necessity to upset the equilibrium I tried so hard to maintain by joking with The Boo. In my initial paranoia, everyone who inhabited the nether regions of Bond Hall, everyone who weighed and measured demerits, and everyone who had any connection with discipline or punishment was anathema. This was the myopic freshmen universe I had created around me. So we moved in different circles and my footwork in avoiding him gradually grew more skillful. Had certain things happened the way they should have happened, we never would have crossed swords, nor would our horns have locked in combat, nor would we have become friends. But in the final days of my junior year, I had become gray enough, in my opinion, to risk adding a dash of color to my bland exterior. The mollusk emerged from his shell for a brief excursion into notoriety. It was the failure of this excursion that brought me before The Boo, the high tribunal of justice who caught me not in my clothes of gray, but in my robes of bright crimson.

It began innocently enough. I was a member of the *Shako*, the campus literary magazine whose primary objective often seemed to be the death of literature rather than the creation of it. Regardless of the merits of the magazine, Jeff Benton, the editor in chief, appointed me poetry editor at the end of my junior year. The position seemed innocuous enough to coexist with the theory of grayness. Everything seemed fine until one sultry April afternoon a surreptitious knock interrupted a daily nap. My roommate, Mike Devito, stopped lifting weights and ushered a rather cadaverous senior, with nervous hands and quick, black eyes, into the room.

He walked to my bed, shot a backward glance at the door, looked at my roommate and said, "Can we trust him?"

Since Mike had returned to his weights, I told the stranger he had nothing to fear from anyone in room 4428.

"I have a poem. I want you to read it."

"OK," I said, flashing the effervescent wit which always stood me in such good stead. I read the poem quickly. Compared to the poetry I was receiving from other cadets, his offering ranked as a minor masterpiece. "Good. We'll print it in the graduation issue."

"You don't see it," he said.

"See what?" I answered.

Then I saw it. The poem I held in my hands was a tersely written, non-rhyming iambic grenade. If you took the initial letter from the seventeen lines, the words "Webb and Tucker suck" slapped you in the face. General Tucker and General Webb reigned as the arch-villains in cadet life at that particular moment in history, and the thought of twisting a secret blade into their backs without their knowledge appealed to me immensely.

"Mum is the word, my fine lad," I said, patting his back. He smiled gratefully and disappeared into the silent afternoon. Mike had just finished his ritualistic twenty bench presses and was starting his squat thrusts when our visitor departed.

The staff's enthusiasm matched my own. Jeff and Rick Campbell, his chief assistant, discussed the pros and cons of putting the poem into the first issue we were to produce as a staff, but cries of freedom of the press and musty quotes from Horace Greeley carried the day. The poem went in. Like the conspirators against Caesar, we vowed absolute secrecy, and like those conspirators we had little insight into the part we played in our own downfall.

The magazine with the "secret" poem emerged from the press two days before graduation. How the word leaked out no one will ever know. But when the magazine hit the post office boxes, about three hundred sniggering, knee-slapping cadets were there waiting to read the latest screw the cadets had inserted into the heart of the Commandant's Department. Rumor has it that a copy of the magazine with the poem circled was delivered to General Harris fifteen minutes after its circulation. Tac Officers read it to each other over cups of coffee in the canteen minutes after it emerged from the post office. Guffaws boomed out of the pool hall; laughter broke the silence of the library and cadets raced from the barracks to pick up their copy of the contraband poem. Jeff Benton said later that he spent much of that day praying, while Rick Campbell merely contemplated the feasibility of suicide. I studied the theory of grayness and wondered what in the hell had happened.

Thus it came to pass that I would meet The Boo under his own rules, in territory alien to me. That night at supper looking up from a plate of hot dogs and sauerkraut, I saw him enter the South Mess Hall. He did not joke with anyone around him. He hunted big game. Near hysteria, I tried to hide behind a pile of sauerkraut which would have dwarfed a small mountain, but when a look of satanic pleasure crossed his face, I knew the reconnaissance mission was over. And here is how it was on a lost day in May when I faced The Boo as Assistant Commandant for the first time.

"Bum, don't say a single world. Start writing and remember Clemson isn't really such a bad place." Then he slapped a piece of paper in front of me. "I want to know everything, Bubba. Your soul is black. Give me names, dates, addresses, and the wedding anniversary of your parents."

"Colonel, you seem to think I've done something wrong," I answered, my voice cracking only slightly.

"I have three ERW's, Conroy, and your guilty name stinks on all three of them."

"But, Colonel, I have been a model cadet in my three years here."

"You have been a bum. You dazzled me with your footwork for a couple of years but I've got your gonads tacked to my desk now and remember, you bum, they've got a great ROTC Program at Clemson."

"Colonel, I hope this misunderstanding will not hurt my chances for Regimental Commander."

"It'll be cleared up when you walk out of here with your bags packed," Boo answered.

"You don't think I have a chance, Colonel?" I was grasping for straws by this time.

"You don't have a preacher's chance in hell, Bubba. The only chance you've got is for the earth to open and swallow you up before our eyes. Now start writing."

I wrote the most nebulous, general, non-implicating ERW ever written. The rights of man and the Bill of Rights figured heavily in my denunciation of a system which did not allow a flavoring of good ole, apple-pie obscenity once in a while. Whatever I wrote, however, remains lost in some impregnable recess of memory which no man shall ever uncover. What sticks in my mind is the blitzkrieg attack The Boo had launched against me in a matter of seconds. The attack left me reeling and stunned, and put me at a crossroads in my Citadel career which led, it seemed, to my iminent departure from the school. The blitzkrieg came in classic Courvoisie fashion: the sudden appearance at the doorway, the eyes swinging over the startled cadets like the beam of a lighthouse across restless waters, the moment of truth when the eyes rested on the proper victim, the quick thrust of the big guns aimed with careful precision at the selected target, and the stern command learned in other wars from other leaders for unconditional surrender.

The Courvoisie weapons of attack were not spared. His eyes were like laser beams, the stentorian voice broke like thunder off the mounds of sauerkraut around me. He was absolutely certain that he had researched his case so thoroughly, collected so much damaging evidence, and prepared such an airtight case that the only task remaining was to pin the struggling butterfly into the display case he reserved in his museum of infamous cadets.

And his cigar. Dark, nauseous cigars almost always dripped out of The Boo's mouth as he made his appointed rounds. Whenever he chewed a cadet out, he used these cigars with diabolical cunning. He never reprimanded a cadet with his cigar more than an inch or two away from the victim's face. As he ranted about the infraction of divine law, he puffed furiously on his cigar. The cadet, traumatized by the voice and frozen by the severity of the moment, had as his main concern the glowing red ash of The Boo's cigar which threatened to make a cinder of any nose or eye it touched. As The Boo left the mess hall that night and friends swarmed around me to offer consolation, my most immediate thought or the one I can remember now most vividly, was gratitude The Boo's cigar did not burn a third nostril into my face.

That night I called my mother and told her to start sending off for college catalogues. In something akin to despair, she wondered how we were to break the news to my father who was stationed in Viet Nam at the time. Dad, like many Citadel fathers, thought the school was created by a special act of God. To tell him I had been given the boot would be like telling him I was the illegitimate son of a communist drug peddler. Mom put up a stiff upper lip, then let me know in definite terms that I had learned no profane language in her household.

The next day the *Shako* staff met at The Boo's office en masse. The gathering had all the trappings of an Irish Wake. None of us smiled, none of us, that is, except The Boo. With few exceptions all of us were reasonably well adjusted cadets, and his pleasure at catching all of us in one large sweep of the dragnet was obvious. He smiled contentedly, puffing as always on a wet, nauseous cigar butt. He then interrogated each of us on the respective parts we had played in the conspiracy. When we left the office, each of us commented on his remarkable ability to pinpoint guilt and ferret out the truth no matter how deeply it lay hidden. His one statement to me, "Bubba, no need to ask you anything. You're in it so deep, Clemson may not take you." My fate seemingly sealed, I awaited the judgment of General Harris and his council of advisors. I waited and waited. School ended and still I heard nothing. None of the staff had been notified of anything. I went to Colonel Courvoisie's house in the middle of the summer and asked him what the story was.

"Bubba, if it was General Clark as President, you would have left campus before the rising sun. General Harris is new—sort of a rookie feeling his way around. I recommended all of you for 3/60, but I don't think you're going to get anything."

"That's great news, Colonel," I exclaimed.

"It's a living, crying shame. You bums broke the rules and come out smelling like a rose

garden, when you should be walking the quad
with a rifle on your shoulder, wearing blisters
on your feet. You got out of this one, but
remember, every time you make a move next
year, my eyes are going to be on you like stink
on manure."

"Yes, Sir."

Luck and timing played a crucial role in my
first encounter with The Boo. He told me later
that a copy of the magazine had been placed in
his hands about eight minutes after
distribution. The ninth minute found my name
written on a pad by his desk as a prime suspect
for investigation. So the poem, conceived as a
secret gesture of defiance, taught me an invalu-
able lesson I was never to forget, a lesson which
saved me from certain expulsion the following
year when Boo tracked me down again—the
lesson was to trust no one, to walk in shadows,
and never to expose your intentions to other
cadets under any circumstances. An extension
of the lesson was to avoid Courvoisie. Behind
the cigar, the booming voice, and the
penetrating eyes resided a competent Assistant
Commandant who took the meaning of
discipline seriously and who performed his
duty with a kind of bloodhound infallibility that
demanded respect from the criminal element in
Citadel society.

The theory of grayness once more held
dominion over my existence. Shell-shocked
from the *Shako* experience, I once more
retreated into my cocoon, firmly convinced I
would never emerge until Graduation Day.
Once more, the chameleon skin fitted me and I
consciously strove to be nondescript and

inoffensive. All would have been fine but for a single event which found my moral sensibilities deeply offended. Had I not become mad as hell and set myself up as a kind of avenging angel for the cause of justice, my journey toward graduation would have been a waltz.

George Owl, "O" Company Commander, was a nice guy with a poor sense of humor. Since most cadets spend half their time teasing other cadets, this could prove to be a serious impediment in the confining surroundings of battalion life. Whenever Mr. Owl walked by a group of Fourth Battalion cadets he generally was met with a chorus of "Hoot, Hoot, Hoot." If he had ignored this unimaginative slur on his good name, the habit would probably have died a natural death. But George faced several problems. His Tactical officer that year was an ambitious, self-aggrandizing officer who exerted a great deal of pressure on "O" Company to perform well in parades, inspections, etc. Most of this pressure fell on George and the strain was beginning to show. When clusters of jocks from "T" Company started chanting, "hoot, hoot," and when sophomores from his own company started doing it behind his back, something had to break. It did.

Fourth Battalion engaged in a battalion owl call on a Thursday night in early May. Owl paled with rage and frustration. His obvious irritation spurred the cadets on. He huffed and puffed, ranted to the crowds, and struck a rather ludicrous posture when he tried to halt the chanting by raising his arm defiantly. The next day proved to be critical in the life of

George Owl, when the pressure finally became too much, and in a moment of supreme frustration, George Owl went momentarily berserk.

. . . Friday afternoon parade with its flurry of banners and strut of the bandsmen responding to the roll of drums, began with its usual precision. The companies marched out impressively, the First Sergeant barking cadence and the guidon fluttering above the marching cadets. Owl stood in front of Third Battalion watching the smaller companies file out to parade. "O" Company would be along in a matter of seconds. He would then lead them out in the field. But as the men from Kilo passed him, a sophomore in the middle of the ranks let out a loud derisive, "Hoot, Hoot." Enraged, Owl wheeled toward the marching company, hoping to spot the offending cadet. All he saw was a cadet in the last rank laughing at his reaction. Without thought and without hesitation, Cadet Owl, Commander of "O" Company, and one of the top twenty ranking officers in his class, took his sword and plunged it into the leg of the sophomore who dared laugh.

The sword went in about an inch of thigh. Needless to say, the sophomore was taken aback, but in the shock of the moment simply marched out to the parade. He never lost step while this strange incident occurred. The moment passed, George cooled off and gamely led "O" Company to the parade ground.

"K" Company Commander swung his men into their appointed slots and waited for Charlie Buzze, the Battalion Commander, to give "order arms." The young sophomore felt something warm on his leg, looked down, and saw that his dress whites were drenched in blood. He prudently posted, walked off the field, and went straight to the hospital. Miss Maloney stopped the bleeding, then patched the wound. No stitches were required.

The timing of this event was important. It came at a time when a series of confrontations between cadet officers and cadet privates left ill-feeling among a large segment of the corps. Several months before, Peter Them, a senior private of gargantuan proportions, had squirted mustard on the chair of Jerry Bayne, a Cadet Major. Bayne rose out of his chair in the mess hall with a great orange blotch staining his otherise flawless appearance. Bayne exchanged words with Them and the result was Peter the Great walking the Second Battalion quadrangle to the tune of sixty tours.

The rift between privates and non-commissioned officers widened when Rodney Engard, a football player with a low-frustration level, picked a cadet sergeant straight up in the air, held him there for several poignant moments, then showed him the way out of the room. A hot young "Tac" smelled Engard blood and demanded Rodney be shown the way out of Lesesne Gate. Debates flourished around campus. Some cadets, primarily officers, felt that Engard should be punished severely. Other cadets, privates, felt the cadet sergeant over-stepped his jurisdiction and that Rodney should have thrown him over the fourth division. So the incident that the Company Commander could solve with a single meeting of the protagonists became a raging issue on campus. Rodney's punishment was a mere 120 tours.

The most amusing incident occurred by accident. A tradition at The Citadel, time honored and rather sacred, took place every March when the seniors went out of wool pants for the last time in their careers. At the final supper in wools the underclassmen ripped the wool pants from the bodies of unprotesting seniors. The result was a motley arrangement of rags and loin cloths draped haphazardly over private and not-so private parts of the body. Pandemonium ruled unchallenged as wool-hungry sophomores pursued giggling seniors over and under tables. War whoops, screams, and the sound of ripping wool added spice to the strange, chaotic ritual of the annual pants-snatching contest. When it was over, seniors sat at the table naked from the waist down.

"This is not military, nor is it dignified," said Jim Probsdorfer, Regimental Commander for the Class of 1967. His staff agreed. So an ultimatum issued from the lofty chambers in Second Battalion said that henceforth no senior shall be forcibly removed from his pants. Cadets grumbled, but Probsdorfer, as all Regimental Commanders, was a kind of surrogate god who held many thunderbolts in his pack of whiteslips. The appointed night came. The Corps, threatened with tours, confinements and/or death, responded very well at first. Even the putrescent wool pants of several senior privates went untouched by glittering sergeants who thought they would be doing The Citadel a favor by destroying them.

It started somewhere in the Fourth Battalion.

Some lad known only to Jesus sneaked a surreptitious hand to the back pocket of some also anonymous senior and ripped the living hell out of his pants. The chain reaction spread throughout the battalion and within seconds every senior in the south mess hall sat admiring his fruit of the looms. Then a kind of rippling hush gripped everyone. Probsdorfer and several of his staff members stood with menacing glares before the rioting battalion. Silence. Probsdorfer walked slowly down the aisle between the kitchen. Waiters scurried out to see what edict he would make to the Fourth Battalion staff, what punishment he would mete out to the offending companies. This impressive display of leadership was so awe-inspiring that no one seemed to notice the huge, weighty figure of John Bowditch, 260 pound behemoth, crawling like a G.I. under barbwire, squirming his way under tables and chairs, positioning himself for the leap which would immortalize his name forever in any discussion of kamikaze maneuvers at The Citadel. Probsdorfer walked slowly, eyeballing the entire battalion, and did not see the huddled, massive figure of Bowditch crouched behind a chair Probsdorfer would have to pass. No one saw Bowditch until he sprang like an overweight leopard and drove a shoulder into the belly of an astonished Regimental Commander. He knocked him through the swinging doors which led to the kitchen, where they disappeared from sight. Seeing the Regimental Commander handled with such impropriety is something like watching the rape of the Pope. A gasp arose, hissing disbelief. Then all was silent. A moment later, Big John emerged. He waved Jim Probsdorfer's wool pants like a victory banner over his head. The place went wild. Chicken bones filled the air. Gobs of mashed potatoes flung by fifty hands landed on chairs and heads. A food fight broke out in full force. Probsdorfer, in probably the most humiliating situation ever encountered by a cadet officer, slinked out of the back door of the kitchen and scuttled to his room. Though Bowditch became an instant folk hero, a sort of Beowulf, this did not prevent him from walking sixty tours for "assaulting and humiliating the Regimental Commander and inciting to riot." So when George Owl stabbed the sophomore private with his sword, the privates of the Corps were more concerned than usual about the punishment the Commandant's Department would recommend. Cadets argued the various aspects of the case. Would the fact that Owl was a Company Commander affect the thinking of the powers who resided in Jenkins Hall? It did. The word spread slowly, but a few days after the parade, a recurrent rumor spread through every room of each battalion: Owl was going to get off scot free, without any punishment whatsoever.

Believing in the natural order of things, I was more astounded than angry. It seemed inconceivable that Owl would not receive even a single demerit for plunging a sword into another cadet's leg. No matter how much pressure he was under, no matter what prior conditions contributed to Owl's actions, I could see no justification in condoning his act completely. The administration merely whitewashed the incident. The sophomore prudently kept his mouth shut after his Company Commander explained the likely consequences if he (the sophomore tried to crucify Owl.

Mike Devito, my roommate, suggested we do something. Bob Patterson and Bob George had come to our room for one of those interminable bull sessions which in retrospect often seem like the most valuable experiences of college life. We discussed every facet of the Owl case, determined that justice was miscarried, and pledged to bring the festering boil to a head. We discussed my harrowing escape of the year before and agreed whatever was done would be done in absolute secrecy, that we four and no one else would know the plans. Before the night had ended, we resolved to write an underground letter.

Bob Patterson dated the Chaplain's secretary, so we had access to a mimeograph machine and an unlimited supply of paper. I wrote a terse, unemotional letter which was intended to arouse the ire of the Corps. I did not intend to turn Fourth Battalion into a vigilante committee—which almost happened. I entitled the letter: The Owl Call. In the purge which took place after distribution, no one managed to save a single copy of the letter. Here is the gist of the letter.

Owl Call

On May 6, 1967, Cadet Owl, a Company Commander, stabbed Cadet Williams, a Private in Company "K." If this offense had been committed in the civilian world, Mr.

Owl would be charged with "assault with a deadly weapon with intent to maim." He could serve up to ten years in a state penitentiary. But he was fortunate enough to have stabbed a private and justice is meted out with greater severity to privates than to officers. Ask yourself this question: if Private Williams had stabbed Captain Owl with a sword, how many hours would he have lasted on The Citadel campus. Private Engard pushed Sergeant Smith and received 120 tours for his efforts. Private Bowditch ripped the pants off Colonel Probsdorfer and received 60 tours for his troubles. Private Them put mustard on Major Bayne's chair and received 60 tours for this indiscretion. Is mustard on pants a more serious offense at The Citadel than blood on pants? The sword is the cadet officer's symbol of leadership, the finite object which sets him above the average cadet. When this symbol is abused so flagrantly and with such vicious results the officer at fault should be required to pay the consequences. The cadet private should be equal to the cadet officer when punished by the Commandant's Department.

A Cadet Officer

Signing the letter "a cadet officer" was Bob Patterson's idea, to throw the scent off me. On the following Thursday, Mike, Bob Patterson and I left the barracks ten minutes before evening formation. Each of us carried massive stacks of letters. We walked nonchalantly, hoping not to attract any attention. We hit the mess hall on the run and spread our propaganda tract as quickly as possible. Within five minutes every table in the mess hall was amply supplied with the first underground letter of the decade. In another minute we stood retreat with our company. We chuckled and grinned to ourselves, as the other companies moved out to mess.

All hell had broken loose in the mess hall when we got there. Some member of battalion staff had read the letter, analyzed the situation and sent out envoys to collect and destroy every copy. But the surge of cadets aborted the effort. Fourth Battalion Staff scrambled like berserk retrievers over the entire north mess hall. But no matter how many letters they collected, almost every table managed to save a bootleg copy for perusal and study. The Cadet Adjutant blessed the food and it was during the meal that the gist of the letter spread like an enveloping flame over a dry forest. At the beginning of the meal, a kind of reflective hush presided, a time for reading and reflection, but the mood became restless and a little dangerous as the meal continued. Fourth Battalion broke out into an explosive chant, "Hoot, Hoot, Hoot." Several tables lifted their knives into the air and left them remained as a symbolic gesture for Cadet Owl to ponder. The Battalion Commander walked among the tables and quelled what appeared to be a certain mutiny of his charges. Owl himself sat throughout the whole meal, head bent over the letter—a study of man in a tight, strangling predicament for which there was no escape. This moment, when I saw

Owl bent over the white sheet of paper which offered his name as a certificate to propitiate my own sense of the way things should be, convinced me that what I had done was extraordinarily cruel, that I had placed a tremendous burden on the shoulders of one whose existence was traumatic enough. As the cries of "Hoot, Hoot" became more pronounced, the more my sense of revulsion toward my own act deepened. No matter what my feelings were, the letter circulated to more and more hands, and I stood helpless, watching the drama I created inflame the emotions of more and more people.

No mutinies occurred, nor did any massive demonstrations rock the tranquility of the campus. The letter generated much debate and perhaps acted as a catalyst to the administration who appointed a board to review the case and offer a solution to General Harris. The Board also proved to be a whitewash job: Owl was reduced to the rank of private, but no other punishment resulted from the trial. In my mind, I still contended the private would not have lasted a single day at The Citadel had he driven a sword into Owl's leg. But the sense of moral justification hardly mattered any longer. Word came through the grapevine that The Boo was breathing down a hot trail and was very close to apprehending the villains.

The group responsible for the letter met in a shadowy conclave to decide what course of action we should take. If The Boo knew anything it did not seem in character that he hadn't confronted us yet. The Corps was notorious for rumors anyhow. Cadets would believe anything as long as a credible story line went along with it. So Bob Patterson suggested we start a series of rumors to obstruct any progress The Boo might make in our directions. We concocted wild, impossible stories: The Regimental Commander wrote the letter to protest an injustice which troubled him greatly; Owl himself, nursing a guilty conscience, wrote the letter to expiate his sins; Owl's roommate wrote the letter for the simple reason he hated Owl's guts and wanted to see him hung on a towering scaffold; General Harris wrote the letter to stimulate debate in the Corps.

As ludicrous as most of these rumors seem, all of them got back to us in one form or another and all of them, so we thought, diverted the bloodhound determination of Boo from homing in on us. When enough rumors had filtered through the barracks and when total confusion seemed to prevail as to the authorship of the letter, and when no solid clues turned up to stare into our eyes, we felt satisfied The Boo or no other power on earth could deduce our guilt or implicate us in any way, shape, or form. Then I got a call from The Boo.

"Come see me, Bubba."

"O.K., Colonel. What about, if I may ask?"

"Just come see me." The receiver clicked at the other end.

Why he wanted to see me I had no idea, but neither was I prepared for his opening remark when I entered his office, fired a presentable salute, and flashed what I hoped was a calm and winning smile. He looked at me appraisingly and then stunned me by saying, "Hoot, Hoot."

"Pardon me, Colonel," I answered, visibly shaken.

"Hoot, Hoot, you bum."

"Colonel, what are you talking about?"

"The letter. I've been tracking down clues all over this campus, Conroy. None of them have led anywhere. This leads me to believe that you wrote and delivered the letter."

"But you have no proof, Colonel. You can't go around accusing people of things without proof."

"Let me tell you something," he said, putting on the sinister face he reserved for particularly somber occasions. "I've had this job long enough where I can smell a rat in an outhouse. The first time I saw this thing, I knew you wrote it. How long it's gonna take me to gather enough evidence to crucify you, I don't know. But I know this, I'm going to get you this time. If they had let me nail you for that poem last year, this never would have happened. Somewhere in the Corps a leak is going to spring and when it does, your jockstrap is going to swing on a nail above my door."

"But Colonel, you are accusing an innocent man."

"Your soul is black, Bubba."

"Colonel, it hurts me to think you have so little faith in my integrity." I was engaged in a give and take battle of words I could little afford to lose.

"No one on this campus is stupid enough to write anything like that, Bubba. Nobody cares that much either. It's going to be funny to watch you packing your bags two weeks before graduation, your friends gathered around you, and a taxi waiting outside the barracks to take you to Clemson."

"You've got a great sense of humor, Colonel."

"No Bubba, I ain't laughing now. But when I catch you, and believe me I am going to catch you, if I have to walk to hell and back to do it, I'm never going to stop laughing."

"Is that all, Colonel?"

"That's all, Bum. Except for one thing."

"What's that, Colonel?"

"Hoot, Hoot."

"Good afternoon, Sir."

When I told Bob and Mike what had transpired in the office, panic was rife in the room. My experience with The Boo the previous year had left me gun-shy and basically unwilling to challenge the fates again. Bob and Mike had no wish to be expelled a couple of weeks away from graduation. So the knowledge that The Boo was sniffing downwind where we stood naked and exposed frightened all of us. We could only wait, however, for the guillotine to find our necks. The letter, its implications and innuendoes, remained in the forefront of campus conversation, and had it not been for a spectacular event, an event which dwarfed the importance of the letter and ultimately caused it to fade from memory, I am certain The Boo would have brought us to justice. But a week after the letter appeared, three freshmen cadets ventured out of the Charleston harbor on a fishing trip, ran out of gas and drifted out to sea on a three day odyssey which pre-empted every other campus thought or consideration. For three days Coast Guard airplanes scanned the waters of the Atlantic in search of the lost boys. Radio bulletins kept Charleston and the rest of South Carolina posted every hour about the failure to turn up any evidence that the cadets were either alive or dead. The campus buzzed with speculation. Civilians joined the search and literally hundreds of ships and boats put to sea to aid in the frantic effort to find the three boys. On the third day, Mrs. Billie Burn, Postmistress and school bus-driver on Dauf-uskie Island, came upon three boys walking slowly down on the dirt road that cut through the thick tangles and dense forest of the island. "You're the boys from The Citadel, aren't you?" she asked. They nodded and the search was ended.

In the uproar caused by the missing cadets, in the frantic effort to find them in thousands of miles of ocean, in the attempt to coordinate the rescue efforts and to satisfy a curious public, The Citadel had no time to think of anything else. The letter was forgotten. We were home free.

On Graduation Day I sought out The Boo and shook his hand. I thanked him for his help and hoped he would call if he ever needed me.

"We graduate some bums from this school. But you're at the top of the list, Conroy." He was smiling.

It gave me measureless satisfaction to look at his great brown cigar and familiar smile, then whisper quietly, "Hoot, Hoot."

The Banishment

It took a long time to happen and it happened very slowly and painfully. But with the change of command, The Boo's days in the Commandant's Department were numbered. In the general housecleaning which takes place whenever a new and potent force sweeps onto a college campus, The Boo became a casualty of change. The Boo became expendable. The new advisors did not admire The Boo's work, felt he was too personal with cadets,and felt he was not tough enough to be an Assistant Commandant. The new broom turned into a powerful vacuum cleaner in the Commandant's Department.

In 1966 The Citadel received an influx of a new breed of Tac Officers. They were generally unsmiling, humorless men whose stolid faces and prognathous jaws implied their solemn dedication to the military. Two of these men were Citadel graduates. Two of these men were goddamn ambitious Citadel graduates. Their names are unimportant. Their importance lies in the discontent they bred at The Citadel. They returned to The Citadel, did not like the way Courvoisie was performing in the Commandant's Department and set out to undermine his position.

Captain Winken and Captain Blinken cited instances where The Boo gave weekend leaves to restricted cadets, where he allowed cadets to go to Charleston during the week for personal business, and where he cut confinements of senior cadets. He was too easy they said. The Tac Officers could not work with him. He was bad for The Citadel. He was anathema to the disciplinary system, and the Jenkins Hall juggernaut could not function smoothly until he resigned, retired, or was fired. They spoke with fervor and conviction when they said The Citadel was going to the dogs, that it just wasn't as good as the old Corps; that unless something was done, The Citadel would sink like a surrogate Atlantis into the froth and swirl of the Ashley River. Winken and Blinken were humorless men and they meant what they said: Get rid of Courvoisie or The Citadel was doomed.

Word spread around campus that a minor revolt was stirring in the modern, antiseptic corridors of Jenkins Hall. Others joined the original conspirators, and suddenly, in a strange reversal, The Boo felt the hounds snapping at his heels. The hounds wore Captain's bars and Major's leaves and their numbers grew under the leadership of the two Citadel graduates. The criterion seemed to be: If the cadets like someone, then he is not performing his duty and must be removed. The main targets stood on the horizon like clay pigeons. Courvoisie and Petit must go became the rallying cry. The wolf pack had discovered the trail. The only thing left was for the quarry to be brought down and devoured.

Not only did Winken and Blinken find allies in Jenkins Hall, they went to the Corps for help. They invited cadets to their offices and flattered

them by confiding their concern for The
Citadel's future to them. They said they were
trying to save The Citadel and they needed
everyone's help. They needed the Regimental
Commander. They got him. They needed the
Regimental Exec. They got him too. They managed to enlist a large percentage of the high
ranking officers. With cocker spaniel eyes and
thumping hearts, they told the story of what the
school was like in the old days, before Courvoisie ruined it. Their grassroots movement
started slowly, but gradually gained momen-
tum and followers. One cadet finally organized
a "Save The Citadel" committee which met in
secret in the reception room at Mark Clark Hall.
Many of the top-ranked cadets in the school
were there. All of them looked serious. All of
them looked as if the weight of the entire school
rested squarely on their shoulders. Everyone
was serious as hell. They discussed the decline
and fall of The Citadel, what could be done
about it, and how a plan could be put into
effect. Most cadets present at the meeting
thought something was wrong with the school
and most of them had remedies of one sort or
another. The cadets in charge of the clandestine
meeting had their own panacea to The Citadel's
problems. Captains Winken and Blinken had
coached them well. The "Save The Citadel"
meeting soon degenerated into a "Get The Boo"
meeting, until John Warley, a hulking jock-
scholar from "T" Company said, "I'll be
damned if I'm going to do anything to hurt The
Boo. He has been good to me and has been good
to every one of you guys. See you later." The
meeting broke up soon afterwards. But

valuable seeds had been sown.

Something happened over the Christmas holidays of 1966 which presaged The Boo's overthrow in 1968. It was The Boo's custom during Christmas to check the barracks for illegal articles or any worn-out clothing the cadets collected during the first semester. Old shoes, perforated socks, diseased shakos, moth-eaten bathrobes—these and other items filled The Boo's annual Christmas package to the poor. Whatever he collected on these forays into the barracks went to organizations which distributed clothing to the poor of Charleston. It became a standard joke around school that if you wanted to salvage your favorite pair of worn-out loafers, then you better carry them home for furlough or hide the hell out of them. At Christmas time, The Boo was very methodical in his search of the rooms. Items the crafty cadet may have kept from the Tac's eyes during room inspection appeared in The Boo's holiday grab-bag when he emerged from the barracks. The annual gathering of cadet refuse was a kind of tradition, that is, until the Christmas of 1966.

The Boo made a real haul this particular Christmas. Old shoes the Salvation Army rejected for the feet of indigents, The Boo threw in the trashcan. Hotplates, televisions, popcorn-makers, barbecues, and other illegal gadgets found their way to The Boo's office. When the cadets returned from furlough they asked each other what The Boo had taken from their room. My roommate lost his pair of raggedy loafers, while I was missing the peppermint-striped, multi-ripped bathrobe that gave me such a rakish, barber-shop look on my jaunts to the shower room. Everything was the way it always was, except with Winken and Blinken. Word emanated from their offices and sifted down through the ranks of the Corps; The Boo is a thief. The Regimental Commander and the Regimental Exec, the two top ranked cadets, under the influence of the two Captains, went to General Harris to express their disapproval. The cadets then presented Courvoisie with a list of items he had stolen from the barracks. The thief was branded. Now it was his move.

The Boo got a list of all the items he had supposedly taken, this list included items that had been missing since the start of the college year. He called each cadet who claimed a loss of property to his office and paid him for his loss. Many cadets refused the money outright. Others took the money gladly. When the final tally was made, The Boo had paid out over three hundred dollars. No ultimatum emanated from the President's Office for The Boo to reimburse the cadets. He did it to vindicate himself from the charge of thievery. It was the first time he had taken illicit articles from the barracks and walked out with a criminal record. The Boo also knew that the battle lines were drawn and that the enemy was not above playing dirty as hell.

Through the remainder of 1967 and 1968, The Boo was marked for elimination. His position as Assistant Commandant was doomed. He had to be removed quietly. It had to be done with patience and subtlety. A power struggle ensued with The Boo carrying a hand of deuces. His formidable enemies held all the trump cards. Boo's power rested with cadets, and in the world of Citadel politics, the cadets and their wishes counted for very little. The anti-Courvoisie contingent grew in power and influence. The powers who resided in Bond Hall whittled away at Courvoisie's job until the position of Assistant Commandant meant little more than a glorified pencil-pusher. The Boo was not allowed to give weekends, check confinements, or go into the barracks. Finally, The Boo was not allowed to have any cadets come to him with problems. The end was in sight.

Soon The Boo received word that he would no longer be Assistant Commandant. The Citadel offered him a choice of three jobs. None of them would bring him into contact with cadets. None of them would entail the prestige or status of Assistant Commandant. And even though most people felt The Boo would retire and move away from The Citadel, he had invested too many years into the college. The love he felt for The Citadel was profound. To the surprise of many he took the job as Transportation and Baggage Officer. His office was in the warehouse, a bland structure at the furthest extremity of the campus. Here, he would have no opportunity to meet and talk with cadets; his presence would hardly be noticed on campus. This self-imposed exile pleased everyone.

The Boo caused no ripples; he bitched to no one. He called the Regimental Commander, Tommy Harper, and the President of The Class of '68 to his office. He wanted no demonstrations on his behalf. He faded out quietly, without fanfare or a last raging malediction against The Citadel.

Betsy Petit was not fired or dismissed. The

Tac Officers hounded her out of the Commandant's Department. They insulted her, embarrassed her, and one of them cursed her. The only woman ever to have a military college yearbook dedicated to her wrote a farewell letter to the Corps and quit outright. With Miss Betsy gone, a Citadel era was over.

So the stories end and the legend of The Boo comes to an abrupt and sudden halt. He still works in the warehouse. He has almost no contact with cadets. On big weekends his house is filled with old cadets who knew him as Assistant Commandant. Last Corps Day over a hundred graduates dropped by to say hello. Every Christmas he receives three or four hundred Christmas cards from former cadets all over the world. He still gets telephone calls from guys in trouble or from guys who still know where to go when they need help. Often a young cadet whose brother carried the legend of The Boo into his home will wander into the warehouse to talk of the old days. And that is what they are becoming. The old days. The forgotten days.

Yet there are those who remember. There are those who think of The Boo as the personification of what is good and valuable at The Citadel, there are those who remember the laughter which followed The Boo wherever he went. The whole tone of this book is sentimental and unashamedly nostalgic. It is difficult to be otherwise. I cannot help but wonder why a man so gifted in dealing with people and so understanding of young men and their problems should be exiled to a job of shuffling baggage and ordering toilet paper. In the process of writing this book I asked several people who work for the Citadel to tell me what they thought about Colonel Courvoisie. "He's Mr. Citadel," one of them said. "He's the greatest man on the campus," said another. Then both of them looked around and whispered with obvious paranoia, "If you quote me, I'll deny every word of it." So let the final message of the book also stand as an epitaph to The Boo's career in Jenkins Hall. And may he know, no matter how small the satisfaction, that many of us look to the past and see him as a great generative, motivating force in our youth. If this is too sentimental, then let it be so. For some of us remember.

Boo's Heroes

Because of actions above and beyond the call of duty, the following cadets earned places of special honor in The Boo's heart.

Class of 1960
H. B. Limehouse, Jr.
H. J. Taylor, Jr.
R. S. Verrastro
E. W. Weeley, Jr.

Class of 1961
J. W. Blankenship
C. Crenshaw
R. H. Hughes
K. J. Justice
D. L. Lubotsky
D. R. Neck
F. W. St. Laurent
G. G. Strickland
J. E. Villafranca

Class of 1962
W. Bowden
G. A. Dixon
W. W. Elliott
S. G. Green
F. C. Hearn
W. J. Odle
W. T. Petersen
A. H. Reeves
W. D. Swift

Class of 1963
M. Abbett
L. C. Bruton

C. C. Burgess III
L. P. Carpinelli
E. C. Carter
R. T. Devens
F. G. Ducker
M. L. Eliades
M. A. Forman
B. Giullian
J. H. Helms
J. Heyman II
C. V. Marcolini
J. E. Misskelly
M. L. Rausenberger
J. M. Sellers
L. L. Smart, Jr.
L. B. Stittsworth
J. T. Vincent
A. R. Weldon, Jr.
M. H. Welsh

Class of 1964
C. A. Boccia
S. C. Brown
D. J. Cooper
C. P. Corcoran
D. G. Davis
R. H. Fletcher, Jr.
J. W. Holt, Jr.
T. B. Huguenin
G. L. Jones

J. T. Marcello
C. W. Martin
D. C. Miller
T. A. Mins
H. M. Mueller, Jr.
L. H. Neville
G. R. Palmer, Jr.
W. R. Penland
E. J. Rabin
A. J. Raffo
W. J. Simchick
J. Simons III
J. W. Spencer
F. M. Warlick
M. A. West

Class of 1965
J. S. Comar
H. T. Combs
B. D. Dargan
C. M. Davis
M. B. Foster
J. B. Grimball
T. C. Hellman
W. C. Kurtz
G. M. Lohmer
T. H. Maybank
J. Maybank
W. C. McKinzie
B. A. Miller
G. P. Montes
R. H. Moore
A. M. Nixon
W. L. Noe III
C. H. Phillips, Jr.
R. E. Pinson
T. T. Prichard
J. D. Rivera
R. M. Siarr
E. N. Stevens

L. B. Strauss
J. P. Thomas
M. C. Traywick
J. P. Tucker, Jr.
J. C. Ventras
C. E. Vickery
S. M. Wasserman
A. W. Wilcox, Jr.
P. R. Yaconelli

Class of 1966
H. G. Adkins, Jr.
P. R. Andersen
J. D. Basto
H. M. Boyd
D. T. Brailsford
D. W. Brown
W. H. Cox, Jr.
T. D. Dodd
E. S. Douglas
W. J. Eskew
M. F. Glass III
W. U. Gunn
S. C. Hall, Jr.
E. S. Holland
H. W. Krauss, Jr.
J. L. Law, Jr.
D. L. Maguire
R. C. May
G. F. McClelland
J. W. McCoy
C. B. McDonald
C. W. McDow, Jr.
L. R. Perella
J. A. Sadler
W. S. Smith III
C. J. Stanton
R. K. Wenhold
H. C. Wheeler
P. E. William

Class of 1967

T. J. Anderson II
C. A. Barron, Jr.
J. W. Bowditch
R. C. Boyd
C. E. Cole
K. M. Darby
J. S. DeBerry
J. M. Devito
G. S. Dewey III
T. L. Dorton
P. G. W. Fetscher
R. C. Fulmer
R. E. George
R. N. Gleason
P. R. Green
A. E. Jones
H. E. Keller
J. L. Kelly III
W. A. Leffler III
W. H. Lovett
N. P. Mellen
J. H. Messervy
R. A. Miller
W. M. Milner
L. R. Moody
T. D. Nelken
W. M. Newell, Jr.
R. W. O'Keefe
R. C. Patterson, Jr.
G. D. Reddick III
R. A. Roberts
J. C. Roland
R. R. Rossell III
D. A. Simon, Jr.
A. J. Sitton, Jr.
M. R. Smith
M. W. Smith
N. J. Stogner

P. F. Them
A. C. Verner, Jr.
D. J. Walker
C. R. Whitlock, Jr.
B. D. Wynn

Class of 1968

M. B. Armstrong
C. E. Ashley
J. M. Bacon III
T. H. Bair
J. W. Blackwell
D. H. Butz II
R. E. Chandler
H. K. Clubb
E. C. Cooper
G. W. Dekle, Jr.
G. S. Eckhardt
J. P. Gaillard III
J. H. Grayson, Jr.
A. R. Heyward III
B. J. Jones, Jr.
D. A. Kerchmar
J. A. Kerchmar
L. L. Korda
L. R. Latini
L. J. Linder
S. D. Kerlin
R. M. Lovelace, Jr.
B. K. Metzger
G. Miller III
J. J. O'Donnell
C. B. Pitts
J. R. Powers
W. W. Russ
S. S. Ryburn
W. M. Shields
E. Smith
L. G. Southard III

J. L. Speicher
R. M. Vipperman
W. M. Wieters
B. H. Windham

Class of 1969
R. M. Bowery
N. A. Davis
T. S. Derrick
E. E. Egg
R. S. Hamilton
C. C. Heyward

H. G. Hiers
T. W. Land
R. S. McKenzie III
J. O. Miller
F. M. Moise III
J. W. Ory
M. W. Pitts
R. E. Riel
W. C. Twitty
D. D. Wheale
C. R. Whealey

By unanimous acclamation of 7 cadet classes, Rhett Perry '64 was the biggest hero during the period Sep. 60—Jun. 67.

By acclamation of their peers the following two cadets were considered to be the most outstanding in character, determination and moral stamina.

F. P. Mood, Jr. 1960
J. C. Warley, Jr. 1967

Boo's Immortals

The Boo's Immortals who conceived and established the Courvoisie Scholarship Fund through contributions from the Friends of The Boo:

Chuck Eiserhardt '68
Mike Runey '68
Tom Linton '68
Randy Heffron '69
Larry Linder '68
P. Gaillard '68

Capers Barr '63
Al Jones '67
Bill Warner '65
Mark Ackerman '67
Jay Keenan '67
Harold Jones '66

Danny Maguire '66
Billy Wieters '68
Pat McGregor '68
Bob Haskins '68
Buzz Glenn '68
Tom Dodd '66
Lloyd Fitzgerald, Jr. '67
Pat Johnson '66
George Munroe '67
Bill Milner '67
Frank Mood '60
Bobby Crouch '62
Stan Hurteau '64
Bill Gunn '66
Wes Jones '68
Gene Morehead '68
Phillips McDowell '70

Herb Koger '61
Ross Cowan '63
Ed Pendarvis '65
Steve Grubb '67
Ephraim Ulmer '69
Frank Gibson '69
Jack West '70
Bill Munday '70
E. F. Hesse, Jr. '69
H. Y. McSween, '67
F. G. West, Jr. '64
T. Lane '68
Johnny Hart '68
Bill Christenbury '67
Witt Smith '66
John McGee '68

And the Class of '38 led by Dr. Henry Rittenberg

Citadelese—Translation of Citadel Terms

"A" company—tall company of undisciplined animals who played footall and basketball. "A" company was generally a military disaster area.

Amnesty—when the President of the College removes all cadet punishment. Murderers, cutthroats, thieves, rapists and cadets are the only people in the world who receive amnesty.

Barracks—place where cadets pretended to live. Four stories of dwellings facing an open quadrangle.

Bluebook—written by Jehovah. The rules and regulations of The Citadel. It appeared to Courvoisie in a grotto near Charleston in the form of a burning bush. The supreme law unto the Corps.

Bond Hall—building where physics professors flunked half the sophomore class. It once housed the Commandant's Department before the move to Jenkins Hall.

Brace—an exaggerated position of standing at attention. Plebes brace. Their chins are tucked in, their shoulders thrown back, and their backs are rigidly straight. When the plebe quits bracing, he is an accepted member of the Corps of Cadets.

Capers Hall—Liberal Arts building.

Clemson—a cow pasture in the upper part of the state.

Confinement—a punishment which required the cadet to sit at his desk studying for two solid hours.

Coward Hall—building where edible food was rumored to be prepared. The mess hall.

DI—Division Inspection. A DI accounted for the occupants of a room at a specific time.

ERW—Explanation Required, Written. Strange military procedure whereby cadets write incriminating documents about themselves.

Five-year man—individual who leisurely strolled through the groves of academe. A true scholar. One who remained in college an extra year to reap the benefits of a Citadel education.

Food fight—odd occurrence which took place in the mess hall, usually during times of frustration or duress. Any type of food could be hurled. Chicken bones very popular. Gobs of spaghetti very popular. Pudding and whipped cream very popular. Everything popular that could become airborne in a moment's notice.

Guidon—split tail flag to identify a company during a parade or drill; also the manual of knowledge for a freshmen; the plebe bible.

Honor system—At The Citadel, the cadet does not lie, cheat, or steal—nor does he tolerate anyone who does these things. The Honor Court tries cadets accused of honor violations.

Jenkins Hall—building where Tactical Officers proved conclusively that the military is not a science.

Jock—a cadet who liked sports better than spit shined shoes.

Johnson Hagood Stadium—where The Citadel football team performs.

Knob, plebe, dumbhead, screw, wad, waste, nut, abortion, fourth-classmen—all euphemisms for freshmen.

Lesesne Gate—if you pronounce this Le-sess-knee, you are not from Charleston. It is pronounced Le-sane and is the main entrance to The Citadel campus.

LeTellier Hall—civil engineering building.

Mess carver—the senior who sat at the head of a table in the mess hall. He was responsible for making sure the meat served to his table was really dead.

Moon shot—exposure of rear end to the general public. Frowned upon by Citadel authorities.

O.C.—Officer in Charge.

O.G.—Officer of the Guard.

Padgett-Thomas Barracks—Second Battalion

where cadets walked punishment tours.

PMS—Professor of Military Science.

Pom-pom—a thing sticking out of a shako; a private's plume.

Pop-off—term used by upperclassmen when they wanted a freshman to speak to them.

Press—a locker where the cadet kept his clothes and personal articles. Civilian equivalent of a closet.

Pulled or burned—term used by cadets to describe the act of giving or receiving demerits. (Seldom used W.P. terms; 'slug a cadet').

Rack—a cadet's bed.

Rack monster—evil, siren-like creature which dwelt under Citadel blankets and caused cadets to answer the call of sleep in lieu of his other duties.

Reconsideration of award—a punishment has been awarded for an offense. The cadet is able to request that the punishment be reconsidered or removed due to extenuating circumstance. These are written when The Boo considers your ERW's bullcrap.

Sallyport—a port or door through which cadets "sallied" out to class or drill. The four main gates to each barracks were called sallyports.

Senior private—a human being resembling a pig. Senior cadets not selected to be officers. Cadets without power who rule the barracks.

Shako—tall, uncomfortable hat worn by cadets during parade and inspection.

SMI—Saturday morning inspection. Cruel ceremony in which Tactical Officers scrutinize the physical appearance of the slobs in their companies.

Summerall Guards—crack drill team that did not walk on water as believed by some of its members.

Sweat party—ceremony where upperclassmen tortured freshmen until sweat poured freely from their bodies. The sweat party is a direct descendant of ancient rituals where virgins were cast into the fire to appease angry gods.

"Tac"—short for Tactical Officer. Army and Air Force officers who came to The Citadel as ROTC teachers and military advisers to cadet companies.

"T" Company—the company of jocks and monsters that made "A" Company look like the Summerall Guards.

The Cid or El Cid—cadet nickname for The Citadel.

Tour—a form of punishment where a cadet had to walk back and forth across the second battalion quadrangle with a rifle on his shoulder. A monumental waste of time.

VMI—a school burned by the Yankees during the Civil War and unfortunately rebuilt soon afterwards.

Waist plate—piece of brass to be worn around the waist during parades and inspection. Waist plates were non-functional and difficult to keep shined.

Week End Leave—(WEL) authorized leave time for a cadet on weekends. Period when cadets become human for brief snatches of time.

West Point—a college north of Slippery Rock.

Whiteslip—a piece of paper used to report a cadet for a disciplinary offense. At the top of the whiteslip is written this immortal epigram, "Discipline is training which makes punishment unnecessary."

BESTSELLING BOOKS FROM TOR